A ROOF OVER OUR HEADS AND FOOD ON THE TABLE

A ROOF

OVER OUR HEADS

AND

FOOD

ON THE TABLE

TED J. BROOKS

LitPrime Solutions
21250 Hawthorne Blvd
Suite 500, Torrance, CA 90503
www.litprime.com
Phone: 1-800-981-9893

Published by LitPrime Solutions   08/11/2022

ISBN: 979-8-88703-031-9(sc)
ISBN: 979-8-88703-032-6(e)

Library of Congress Control Number: 2022913021

DEDICATED TO

JASON

CONTENTS

CHAPTER ONE

As a Newcastle High School senior, Pat Kavanaugh waited for the day when his acceptance letter would come from Nutmeg State University, located in Millbury, Connecticut. On the day following Easter, his mother, Maureen, handed him the bulky envelope containing the good news. Pat quickly opened it and read the acceptance letter quietly. After he read it, he showed it to his mother. He also flipped through the course catalog that was included.

"I'm sure your father will be proud of you!" she announced.

While Pat and his parents were having dinner, he said, "I've been accepted as an undergraduate student at Nutmeg State University for the fall, Dad."

"That's terrific, son!" His father, John Kavanaugh, said as he picked up a piece of bread and spread butter on it. "What are your thoughts regarding a field of study?"

"I'm thinking of being an English major. I want to be a writer."

"A writer? That's not very practical. That kind of work will not give you a steady paycheck every week." His father's face changed from smiling to almost turning the color of beets. "The only kind of writing that I know of is freelance, and, you wouldn't get paid on a regular basis. You need the kind of job that puts a roof over your head and food on the table. You should find a job that would provide you with a sense of financial independence."

"There are other ways a writer can have a job that provides a weekly paycheck, such as being a reporter for a newspaper, Dad."

"I still think that kind of work will lead you to times of feast or famine, Pat," his father replied.

"What your father is trying to say is that he wants only the best for you. He doesn't want you to go for weeks living hand to mouth. We are under the impression that if you graduate with such a degree, you will have a difficult time trying to find a job in that fi eld. We are trying to make it easy for you so that you wouldn't have to struggle, Pat," his mother said gently. "Since you're good with numbers, did you ever think of accounting?"

"Accounting would be a career that would enable you to get a well-paying job, with weekly paychecks, medical and dental insurance, and a retirement plan. You would let your employer take care of those benefits for you. All you would have to do is show up for work, do your job, and then go home at the end of the day," his father said. "An honest day's pay for an honest day's work, my father used to say."

"Your grandfather had a tough time making ends meet in the years of the Great Depression. There would be months that he didn't have any income at all. How he got through it all was a mystery to me, but his experiences are something we don't want you to go through," his mother said.

"I don't like the idea of putting nice little numbers into nice little boxes," Pat protested. "Not another word about it. You're going to major in accounting because we're paying for your tuition. Have I made myself clear about it?" his father demanded. "If you do what I say, you'll be set for life. A career in accounting will provide you with stability for the years that you will be working until you are ready to retire. You don't want to be struggling at that point, scrambling for a comfortable retirement. I don't want you to go through what my father experienced."

"Yes, Dad," Pat said dejectedly.

"We have decided on accounting for your major because we know what's best for you, our son," his mother said quietly.

After Pat graduated from Newcastle High School, he made plans during the summer for his first year of life at the university. For example, the university administration assigned him to an advisor named Dr. Williams, who invited him to get acquainted with her. Two weeks before the first day of classes, Pat made an appointment to see Dr. Williams. Getting on the Constitution State Turnpike, he drove south through Mapleton. After the sign on the side of the highway with the words, "Entering Millbury," he saw another sign that featured the logo of Nutmeg State University: the words of the university arranged in a circle, with the outline of the State of Connecticut in the middle. The sign had the words, "This Exit," below the logo.

Pat took the exit and went down the ramp. As he stopped, he saw the sign for the university pointing to the left and went in that direction. Continuing for about two miles down University Avenue, he passed All Saints' Church, with its steeple rising in the sky. He knew that he would go to that church for Mass on Sundays. One of the unspoken concerns his parents had was whether he would continue attending Mass on a weekly basis. Across the street from All Saints' Church was the cemetery for its parishioners. Pat decided that he would like to walk through it someday.

About a half-mile past the church was the NSU campus. Occupying the left side of University Avenue were the university grounds, stretched out on a block of land between Nutmeg Lane and State Street. The administration building, facing University Avenue, had two floors and a bell tower with a clock on all four sides; it soared into the sky. On the corners of both side streets were the signs indicating the entrance to NSU.

Pat drove on Nutmeg Lane and found a parking space in the visitors' area, according to Dr. Williams' directions that he'd received earlier. He made his way to the Administration building and went to the reception area. The receptionist greeted him by saying, "Good afternoon. May I help you, sir?"

Pat replied, "I have an appointment with Dr. Williams. Do you know where I may find her?"

"Which Dr. Williams?"

"She is my advisor for accounting, ma'am."

"The Accounting Department is located at Harriet Beecher Stowe Hall. Here is a campus map for you." She gave him a copy of a map that displayed the various buildings of the NSU campus, bearing the names of the famous literary figures of Connecticut.

"Thank you, ma'am," Pat said as he left the Administration building. He followed the sidewalk to Harriet Beecher Stowe Hall. Inside the lobby was a directory. The first floor contained the classrooms, with the second and third floors were reserved for the professors' offices. After locating Dr. Williams' name on the directory, he climbed to the second floor, and found Dr. Williams' office. He knocked on the door.

A woman's voice said from inside, "Just a minute." Pat waited patiently but felt a little unsettled. This relationship between him and his advisor would either make his career or break it, but it was something he would have to get through one way or another. The heavy wooden door opened, and Dr. Williams stood in the entrance. She was five-feet-seven, with graying blond hair, half-moons on a string on her neck, and little makeup. Dressed professionally, she conveyed that she was all business for academia. "Pat Kavanaugh?" she asked as she held out her hand for him to shake. "It's a pleasure to meet you. We have the next four years together, which I hope will be memorable for you."

"Yes, Doctor."

"None of this Doctor stuff. Call me Liz." She smiled charmingly, her features slowly relaxing. "I may have a Ph.D. in accounting, but I am a regular person just like you." She welcomed him into her office and shut the door. "Have a seat in front of my desk," she said as she sat across her desk from him. Behind her was a large window, which looked out into the campus grounds. Opening a file cabinet, she withdrew a folder from it. It had his name printed on the tab. She opened it on her desk and slipped her half-moons onto the bridge of her nose. "I have a copy of your high school transcript. Very impressive: all A's and B's. You even graduated in the top ten percent of your class. I also have a copy of your SAT scores and your application to NSU." She slid her half-moons onto the top of her head. "Why accounting?"

"It's what my parents want."

"But what do you want?" "I wanted to major in English."

"But your parents evidently disapproved of that idea." Pat was surprised. "How did you know?"

"I get a lot of students who were pushed into this field because it's something 'practical.' They'd rather do something that's not very realistic, like theatre or art or my personal favorite, philosophy. I've seen it all. If that's what your parents want, and evidently, they are paying the tuition, then it's my job to see you through it."

"I was feeling unsure about the idea myself," he said as he broke into a smile.

"Here's what I'll do. As your advisor, I will make the schedules for you and be in touch with the instructors on a weekly basis. Of course, if you think you are having a problem, then I'll arrange for some private tutoring. What am I doing for you isn't the norm for students at the university, so we'll just keep it between us."

"I was wondering if I will be able to live on campus, Liz."

"I'm glad you asked. I also have arranged with the Residential Life Office so that you don't have to commute back and forth from home. You will move in on Labor Day. I don't have any other information right now, but I requested that you live in one of the male-only dormitories."

"And the meal plan?"

"All set as well. You will show your student ID to the staff member. Do you have time to get one today?"

Pat nodded. "Yes, I can get one this afternoon."

Liz stood up, indicating that the orientation session was over. Pat rose to his feet and she escorted him to the hallway. With another firm handshake, she said, "Welcome to Nutmeg State University."

"I am looking forward to perhaps the best four years of my life, Liz," Pat said as he stepped into the corridor. He continued walking out of the building. Before going to his car, he had his photo taken for his ID. After he received it, he went to his car in the parking lot. He knew that his father would be pleased as punch to know that his life was coming together. The guidance that Dr. Williams offered to him would be handy, Pat thought as he drove along the Turnpike to go home.

In his orientation packet, Pat read that his residential hall staff was expecting him to move into the dormitory on Labor Day, because classes were beginning on Wednesday. After a last hearty, home-cooked breakfast, he packed everything he was going to need for the next three months until the Christmas break: clothes, grooming supplies, an assortment of books, tapes and CDs, as well as notebooks, pens and other classroom items. It all fit into the one steamer trunk that he had. When he was packed, he told his parents, "I'm off to NSU, Mom and Dad."

"Give us a call, honey," his mother said as she watched him open his car door and get behind the steering wheel. "Let us know how you're doing."

"Okay, Mom and Dad". I'll call on Sunday night," Pat said after he rolled down his window. Then he rolled it back up and honked his horn and waved as he backed out of the driveway and drove to the university, which would be his home for the next four years.

He parked his car in the appropriate parking lot. After attaching the required bumper sticker, he went to the Residential Life Office located in the Administration building. He opened the door and approached the staff member behind the counter.

"May I help you, sir?" she said. "Yes. I'm Patrick Kavanaugh."

The staff member entered his name into her computer and then printed a sheet of paper for him. "Here's all the information you need to get settled in as on-campus resident."

She handed him the sheet. "When you go to Clemens Hall, you will get your key."

"Thank you, ma'am," Pat said as he placed the keys in his pocket, left the office and went to his car. He took out his trunk and carried it to Clemens Hall. He opened the door and brought his trunk inside. He saw a man, the dorm director, at a counter in the lobby. He went over and introduced himself.

"Pleased to meet you, Pat," The man said. "I'm Tom Hoskins, the dorm director. You'll be in room 243, and your roommate is..." Tom looked at his sheet that listed the residents' names and their assigned rooms, "...Sean Donnelly."

"Is Sean here yet?" "No." "May I have my key?"

"Absolutely, Pat. Welcome to Clemens Hall." Tom handed him the key to his room. "Please don't lose this."

"Thank you, Tom." Pat took the key from him and carried the trunk to his room on the second floor. Finding the room, he unlocked the door and put his trunk down before entering it. The furniture in the room consisted of two beds, two nightstands, two desks and two bureaus. A window at the far of the room overlooked a view of the campus. Pat brought in his trunk and placed it on the floor. The first thing he did was choose the bed closest to the door. That was his personal preference, based on his experiences as a child. He first put a pad on the bare mattress and over that a fitted sheet. Then he tucked in a flat sheet and a blanket before placing on top the bedspread. He also put a pillow inside a matching pillowcase.

Then he chose one of the bureaus and placed his clothes inside it. While engrossed in this activity, he was caught off-guard when he saw the door open. A tall student with blond hair entered.

"Hello. You must be Pat Kavanaugh. I'm Sean Donnelly."

"Yes. I'm Pat. Nice to meet you," Pat said as he stood up and held out his hand to Sean. "Are you a first-year student, Pat? I am."

"Yes, Sean."

"I see that you started putting your things away," Sean said as looked around.

"Did you mind me choosing a bed or a bureau, Sean?" Sean shook his head. "It really doesn't matter to me at all." He began making his bed. When he was finished, he put his clothes into the other bureau. Sean said, "I'm from Winston, in the southern part of the state."

Pat replied, "I'm from Newcastle. It was originally known as Newgrange Castle, a section of Millbury. The Irish immigrants from County Meath settled it in the 1840s, fleeing the potato famine. The name was derived from Newgrange, which is a prehistoric site in the area. It's a passage tomb. Because these people were finally free from being subjected to the British Crown, they felt that their own houses would be castles, hence the 'castle' part. In 1925, Newcastle was incorporated as a separate municipality. Both of my parents are descended from the original settlers."

"I'm also of Irish ancestry, Pat," Sean replied. "My ancestors came from County Donegal. A few of my uncles are police officers."

"Do you plan to follow in their footsteps?"

"I don't think so, Pat. It doesn't appeal to me."

"I'm glad that we share the same ethnic heritage, Sean," Pat smiled. Let's call ourselves the Hibernian Brothers!"

Sean announced, "I took Latin and I know that was the word the Romans used to describe the Irish people. To the Hibernian Brothers! Sláinte!" He raised an imaginary glass, as if making a toast.

Pat smiled when he heard that expression. He vividly recalled a pleasant memory of his parents and their friends toasting each other with bottles of Guinness beer, exclaiming, "Sláinte!" at the top of their lungs. He remembered that Sláinte means "to your health" in Gaelic.

After they finished arranging their room, they decided to go to the dining hall for their first taste of college food. After showing their student IDs to the staff associate, they entered the serving line. They each took a tray, a glass, silverware and napkins.

"What looks good to you, Pat?" Sean said as he surveyed the entrées being served: macaroni and cheese, spaghetti and meatballs, fish and chips, and countless other choices. There was also a salad bar in the middle of the serving area, featuring fresh greens and vegetables, accompanied by fresh fruits, gelatin cubes, dressings, bacon bits and croutons.

"I'm having spaghetti and meatballs, Sean," Pat said as he accepted the dish from the server.

"I think a slice of Italian bread would go fine with this." He placed the dish on his tray and moved down to the bread display. Taking a slice of Italian bread, he placed it on his tray and a pat of butter. He filled his glass from the dispenser of soft drinks.

Sean chose the fish and chips, accompanied by a small dish of cole slaw. He also filled his glass with his favorite soda. Taking their trays to an empty table by a window overlooking the other campus buildings, they sat down. Pat slathered butter on his piece of bread before diving into his spaghetti and meatballs.

"What's your major, Sean?" Pat asked.

"It's mathematics. What's yours?"

"Accounting. My father wanted me to be an accountant because it's practical. He thinks by being one I'll have a steady job for the rest of my life. But I don't find the work of putting nice little numbers into nice little boxes to be thrilling."

After they finished eating, they went back to their room. At seven in the evening, Sean said, "Do you mind if I turn on my TV? There are two game shows that I like watching. Then from eight until ten I like to watch the prime-time sitcoms that are on."

Pat said, "Not at all. I like watching those shows."

Sean smiled. "I knew that we would get along very well. We have a lot in common. I'm so glad that we are roommates," he said as he turned on his TV and tuned to the channel that had the game shows. Then he sat down on his bed. Pat also sat on his bed, and they spent the next three hours watching TV. At ten in the evening, Sean stood up and turned off the TV. "I'm ready to go to bed now." He unlaced his sneakers and pulled off his socks before pulling his shirt over his head and unzipping his jeans. Clad in only his boxer shorts, he pulled back the bedspread and slid under the bed sheet and blanket.

"You just wear boxers, Sean?" Pat said as he undressed and then put on his pajamas. Then he switched off the overhead light, plunging the room into darkness. Then he pulled back the covers of his bed and slid under them, pulling them over him.

"I'm more comfortable this way," Sean said. He rolled over onto his side, facing the window. "So what time do you want to wake up in the morning?" Pat asked.

"Around eight. We can have breakfast before going shopping for books. "Good night, Pat."

"Good night, Sean," Pat said before closing his eyes. Within minutes, they fell asleep.

CHAPTER TWO

At eight-thirty in the morning, Pat woke up. He saw that Sean was still sleeping, so he lay in his bed quietly. Placing his hands under his head, he stared at the ceiling, focusing on the tiles above him. He was thinking about university life: studies, the other students, and the professors. He also had the hope that he would land a full-time job with the benefits and a retirement plan. He felt his father would be very disappointed with him if he graduated with a degree in accounting and not be able to secure a lifetime of employment.

While Pat was thinking about these ideas, he noticed that Sean was opening his eyes and throwing back the covers to get out of bed. "Good morning, Pat. Did you wake up before I did?"

"Yes, Sean, I was awake for about a half hour. Do you want to take a shower? I'll stay here until you come back from the men's room."

"Thanks, Pat. I won't be long." Sean grabbed a towel and threw it around his neck. Then he located his can of shaving cream, his razor, and a bar of soap. He walked down the hallway to the men's room to take a shower. He found an empty stall, turned on the water, dropped his boxers and enjoyed the spray of water on his face, his shoulders and on his back. Rubbing the soap bar along his chest and across his arms, his thoughts focused on how happy he was to have Pat for a roommate.

It seemed to him that because they were both of Irish descent, they had a lot in common, and he was glad that they were getting along very well.

Turning off the water, he stepped out of the shower stall and rubbed his chest and back with his towel before putting on his boxers. Then he went to the row of sinks in the men's room and stood in front of one of them. He splashed warm water on his face before applying shaving cream to it. Looking at himself in the mirror, he used his razor to shave his face. After shaving, he put an aftershave lotion on his face before going back to his room. "I'm all done, Pat. You can take a shower now."

"Thanks, Sean," Pat said as he gathered his grooming supplies and his towel. After taking a shower, he also shaved his face and then returned to his dorm. Sean was already dressed when he came in. "After I get dressed, we can go have breakfast before going to the bookstore, Sean."

While Pat was in the men's room, Sean decided to impress Pat by wearing a white short-sleeved shirt that bore the Donnelly family coat-of-arms. When Pat came into the room, Sean said, "What do you think of my shirt?"

"I'm glad you are showing off your heritage, Sean! I have a similar shirt also!" Pat located a similar shirt that had the Kavanaugh family coat-of-arms. He put it on before going to the dining hall.

After a hearty breakfast, Pat and Sean went to the State Street Bookstore. They each took a shopping carriage and set off to buy the required textbooks that their professors were using in their courses. After Pat finished loading his carriage with his books, he said to Sean, "I'm all done. I'll see you in the dorm." He headed for the checkout.

Sean replied, "Okay, Pat. I'm going to look around at the magazine rack before I check out. See you later." After Pat left the State Street Bookstore, Sean lingered at the magazine rack. His attention was drawn to the buxom blonde in a tight bikini adorning the cover of *Playboy* magazine. He knew that she would be featured sans bikini as the Playmate of the Month. As he went to pick it up, and look at it, he heard his mother's strong admonition echoing in his ears: *If you look at pictures of naked women, you will go blind.* He put it back. As he returned it to its place, he noticed a magazine next to it. The magazine's cover featured a bare-chested man with black hair and a thick black mustache. There was a smoldering look in his dark eyes. The man's mouth was set not in a smile, but in a sneer, as if to entice the reader to view the rest of his body. The hair on the man's chest was thick as it cascaded around his nipples before tapering to a thin line to his belly button. The man's jeans were unbuttoned, exposing the waistband of his underpants. Then Sean looked at the title of the magazine. He had never heard of this magazine before. Unlike *Playboy*, which was in a sealed plastic bag, the magazine was not protected as such.

Looking over his shoulder to make sure that no one was watching him, Sean lifted it from the rack and sneaked a peek at the centerfold. The model featured on the cover was displayed in his birthday suit, with nothing left to the imagination. Sean decided that he had to buy the magazine, because he realized instantly that he appreciated the visual splendor of male nudity. Besides, he thought to himself, Mom never said I would go blind from looking at pictures of men without their clothes on. Carefully closing the magazine so that no one else saw him looking at it, he placed it under the textbooks that he was purchasing, and he pushed his carriage to the checkout area.

Sean was grateful that he was the only one checking out. He placed his books on the counter and waited for the cashier to begin ringing his sale.

"How are you doing, sir?" the checkout operator said as he waved his wand and scanned the UPC codes on the textbooks.

"Okay. This is my first year at NSU." "I'm a senior. Anything else before I complete your sale?" "Yes. I'd like to buy this magazine." Sean placed the magazine on the counter. The cashier was astonished that a male student would want to buy a magazine that featured nude guys. "Are you sure you didn't make a mistake? You are supposed to want to look at pictures of nude women, not guys with their clothes off." "So you're saying is that it's wrong for a man to see other men in the buff." "Yes, that's exactly my point." "I really would like to buy this magazine, and I don't need a hassle. As they say, the customer is always right," Sean forcefully made his point.

The cashier was taken aback by this show of bravado. "I'm sorry, sir, that I gave you a hard time. I was just caught off-guard. Here, let me put it in a bag by itself to protect your privacy." He gingerly took the magazine and bagged it separately from the rest of Sean's textbooks. Looking at his cash register display, he said, "Your total is $325.47, including sales tax."

Sean handed him a stack of twenties and a ten. The cashier made change for him, consisting of three pennies, two quarters, and four ones. "That's three hundred twenty-six, twenty-seven, twenty-eight, twenty-nine, and thirty. Thank you for shopping at the State Street Bookstore, sir. Have a good day." The cashier then gave him his receipt.

Sean left the store and returned to his dorm, carrying his bags. He opened the door of his room and saw that Pat wasn't in yet. Breathing a sigh of relief, he put his bags on his desk. He sat at his desk and took out all his textbooks, and placed them standing up against the wall, as if they were in a bookshelf. Then he placed the bag containing the magazine inside a desk drawer. I'll look at it later, he thought to himself, as he lay on his bed and closed his eyes. He noticed that Pat wasn't back yet. Then he went to lunch by himself, then came back to the room, and lay on his bed for an afternoon nap.

At five in the afternoon, Pat entered the room. "Hey, Sean. Ready for dinner?" He placed his books on his desk. Sean opened his eyes and stood up. "I guess so."

The two roommates left their room and walked to the cafeteria. They got into the serving line with their trays and made their choices from a wide selection of dinner items: spaghetti and meatballs; fish and chips; and country-fried chicken with baked potatoes. There were also soups to choose from and a salad bar. Pat chose fish and chips; Sean decided on spaghetti and meatballs. They took their trays to a table overlooking the campus grounds. While they ate, Pat talked nonstop about his classes, but he noticed that Sean seemed preoccupied. "A penny for your thoughts."

Sean didn't realize that he was lost in thought until Pat spoke. "What?"

"I've been speaking to you for the last five minutes. Didn't you hear a word I said?"

"No. I guess I had a lot on my mind. Sorry if I wasn't paying attention."

"Maybe it's just first-year nerves." Pat theorized. He finished eating his fish and chips. "I'm all done eating. How is your spaghetti?"

Sean lifted a hefty portion to his mouth. He savored the taste of homemade pasta combined with the fresh sauce. "It's delicious, Pat!" "After you are done eating, we'll go back to the room," Pat announced. After Sean finished his last mouthful, they stood up, pushed in their chairs, picked up their trays and brought them to the staff attendant who was supervising the cafeteria.

On the way to their dorm, Pat said, "My first class is at eight in the morning. When is your first class, Sean?"

"Mine is also at eight."

"How about we get up tomorrow at six-thirty, have breakfast at seven-thirty, and then go to class?"

"Sounds like a good idea to me, Pat," Sean replied. "Do you want to watch TV?"

"Sure, Pat. And then we can go to bed at ten."

When they reached their dorm, Pat turned on his TV set and they sat on their beds, watching two game shows and four half-hour sitcoms. After the shows were over, Pat turned it off and they got ready for bed.

On Wednesday morning, they woke up to the buzz of the alarm clock at six-thirty. Pat reached over, shut the alarm off, and yawned. "Sean, I am going to take a shower first." He got out of his bed, gathered all his grooming supplies and threw a towel around his neck. "When I'll come back, you can take your shower."

"Okay, Pat." Sean decided that he was going to sneak a look at his magazine. He got out of his bed, still in his boxers, and sat at his desk. Opening the drawer where he had hid it, he removed it from the plastic bag and flipped to the centerfold. The model featured on the cover was depicted in his birthday suit facing the camera. Unlike the playmates of the month in *Playboy* who were wearing outfits that emphasized their breasts, crotches and rears in the centerfold, the guy left nothing to the imagination. Sean took the time to study the man's physical characteristics. Sean didn't feel rushed as he perused the magazine, as opposed to looking at it before he bought it the day before.

The model was photographed standing up on a beach, with the waves crashing in the Pacific Ocean. He had his hands folded behind his head, exposing his underarm hair. Sean noticed that the man's crotch was lily-white, and his tan lines were apparent. The contrast between the color of the man's groin was significant compared to the tan on the rest of his body. Sean thought that that the reason the man's groin remained lily-white in stark contrast to his suntan was that he wore a bathing suit on the beaches of California. Only those intimate with him were privileged to see him nude. The model's penis was limp as it pointed to the ground, with dark pubic hairs surrounding it. The man's testicles were also visible as well.

Sean also looked at the rest of the centerfold's layout. Along with the photographs was the copy that described the centerfold's background, such as how many girlfriends he had and what his aspirations were. Sean knew that the copy was strictly for the fantasy of the reader and not meant to be taken seriously. The layout began with the model featured in a three-piece suit, sitting backwards on a desk chair in an office. In the background, behind the model, were pieces of office equipment: a computer, a printer, and a fax machine. Then each photo depicted the model in a progressive strip sequence. First, the model removed his suit jacket, unknotted his tie, and unbuttoned his dress shirt. In the second photo, he was photographed wearing only his dress pants. In the third photo, the model was featured in his underpants. The last photo before the centerfold was a full page of the model in his birthday suit.

Sean then flipped through the rest of the magazine. In addition to the various columns and erotic stories from the woman's point of view, there were photos of nude guys. Some were white, some were black, and some were of Asian origin. Some had mustaches, some had beards, and some were cleanshaven. Some had hair on their chests, some had hairless chests, and some were bodybuilders. After Sean was finished looking at it, he put the magazine away in a drawer in his desk and then lay on his bed under the covers. He didn't want Pat to see him reading it. If it were discovered, he was aware that he might be ostracized for it, and he didn't want to take that chance. Sean found himself hard down there.

When Pat was finished with his shower, he entered the room to find Sean lying in his bed. "Okay, Sean, it's your turn." "Thanks, Pat." Sean climbed out of his bed, wondering if Pat could see his erection. His roommate was busy getting dressed, so he didn't notice Sean's bulge in his boxers. Sean threw a towel round his neck, grabbed a bar of soap, his can of shaving cream and a razor, and headed for the men's room.

Once Sean reached the men's room, he relieved himself immediately, and he felt his erection going down. Then he located a shower stall, turned on the water, and removed his boxers. Stepping inside, he closed the shower curtain and relaxed as the water sprayed over his body. He rubbed a soap bar over his chest, while thinking about the nude guys he saw photographed in the magazine.

After his shower, he dried himself off and put his boxers on. He then approached the row of sinks. Looking into a mirror above one of the sinks, he splashed warm water on his face before applying shaving cream to it. After he shaved, he returned to his room and put on a pullover short-sleeved shirt and a pair of jeans. Then he put his required textbooks and a notebook into his book bag. Pat placed his book bag on his desk and sat in his chair while waiting for Sean.

"Ready for breakfast, Sean?" Pat said when he saw that his roommate was ready.

"Yes, Pat." They locked their door and went to the dining hall. Getting into the serving line, they preferred pancakes and bacon instead of cold cereals. Pat also chose to have a cup of black coffee without sugar or cream.

"How can you drink it like that?" Sean asked as he saw Pat lift the coffee mug to his mouth. "I would need to doctor it with at least half-and-half in order to drink it." "You don't know what you're missing!"

"I suppose so, Pat. I don't think I can acquire a taste for it. Anyway, what do you have for classes this morning?"

Pat looked at his schedule taped to his notebook. "Let's see. I have world history at eight, first-year composition at nine, and introduction to accounting at eleven."

"I have a math class at eight, biology at nine, and introduction to theater at ten. Then I have the rest of the day free."

"So we'll get together for lunch at noon, after my accounting class," Pat said as he polished off his coffee. "Let's go to class." They stood up, pushed in their chairs, and brought their trays to the staff attendant supervising the students.

As they walked down the steps from the dining hall, they came to a sidewalk. At that point, they went off in opposite directions. "See you later, Sean," Pat said as he went to his first class.

"Okay, Pat." Sean went to his first class.

After Pat's accounting class, he met with Sean in front of the dining hall. "How were your classes, Pat?" Sean said as they walked up the stairway.

"It was okay. The high point was in the first-year composition class. The instructor gave us a quiz on thirty of the most misspelled words, and we had to determine if the word was correctly spelled, and if it wasn't, we had to provide the correct spelling. Some students were upset because they thought that some of the words were misspelled, when they were spelled correctly," Pat said as they got into the serving line.

"That was tricky." Sean took a tray, silverware, a napkin and a glass.

"You're telling me!" Pat said as he also took a tray, silverware, a napkin and a glass.

"How did you do?" Sean asked while he pointed to a server that he wanted macaroni and cheese.

"I got a B-," Pat said as he accepted from the employee behind the serving counter the soup of the day: cheddar cheese with broccoli.

They took their trays to a table and sat down. Pat asked, "How were your classes?"

Sean replied, "They were okay. I really enjoyed the theater. The instructor is funny. She had us in stitches with her stories about what happened behind the scenes. I can't recall much of what she said, but I found the class to be the most enjoyable." Sean started eating his macaroni and cheese. He then remembered that he had the magazine in his desk. *I hope no one finds it*, he thought to himself as he ate his lunch.

"Do you plan on going to church on Sundays, Sean? I don't really want to attend the nondenominational service held in the Student Union," Pat asked.

"Where do you want to go?" "All Saints Church. It's on University Avenue. I saw on it when I drove by it to NSU."

"Sure. I'd like to go there with you."

"After lunch, we'll go to the Student Union to see if they have a church schedule available." Pat finished his cheddar cheese soup with broccoli. "Ready to leave, Sean?"

"Yes, Pat." Sean said as he put his fork on the plate. They stood up, pushed in their chairs and brought their trays to the staff attendant.

They walked to the Student Union. On one of the walls were schedules for the local churches and synagogues. They found the one for All Saints Church. Pat said, "They have a Vigil Mass at five-thirty on Saturday afternoon, then the Sunday morning Masses are at eight, nine-thirty and eleven." "How about we go to the Vigil Mass on Saturday afternoon?" Sean suggested. "Then we can go to supper after Mass. On Sundays we can sleep in, and not have to worry about missing it."

"I think that's a good idea, Sean," Pat said as they left the Student Union and went to their room. When they reached it, Pat said, "I am going to take a nap before dinner." He lay on his bed and closed his eyes.

When Sean saw that Pat was asleep, he felt he could look at his magazine. He went to his desk and pulled out the drawer containing it. Looking over his shoulder to make sure that Pat was still sleeping; he placed it on his desk and glanced through it. After ten minutes of looking at the photos, he heard Pat getting up from his bed. Quickly Sean placed the magazine in his desk drawer and slammed it shut.

"What's that?" Pat said when he saw Sean shut the desk drawer.

"What's what?" Sean asked innocently. He put his hand on the drawer to prevent Pat from opening it. "I saw you put something in your desk drawer. I want to know what it is!"

"No, you don't!" "Yes, I do!" Pat placed his hand on Sean's wrist and forced him to open the drawer. When he saw the magazine, he said, "Oh, no!" "Aren't you sorry you had to see what it was?" Sean said. He closed the drawer quietly.

"Sean, are… you… gay?" Pat took a pause between each word because he was caught off-guard by this discovery.

"No. Yesterday when I was shopping, I saw the magazine and realized that I like looking at photos of male nudes."

"Male nudes, naked guys, you've seen one man without his clothes on, you've seen them all. Besides, you're supposed to be buying *Playboy*."

"When I was sixteen, an older friend of mine gave me a carton of his old *Playboy* magazines. My mother found them and threw them out. She also told me that if I looked at pictures of naked women, I would go blind." "And you believed her?" Pat burst out laughing. "She was just trying to frighten you from experiencing an adolescent rite of passage." He couldn't believe how gullible Sean was to believe such an outright lie.

"Then my mother told me that I had a dirty mind for looking at pictures of naked women. I have always believed that the human body is a work of art. I didn't think looking at that magazine was a sin."

"Evidently you and your mother have a difference in opinion, Sean," Pat said.

"I just found the whole event to be upsetting. Yes, I did believe her. I was so scared that when she found my stash that I took her words at face value. But she never said I would go blind if I looked at pictures of guys without their clothes on. Yesterday when I was shopping for my textbooks, I stopped by the magazine display. I looked at the magazine and I realized that I appreciated the aesthetic beauty of the male nude."

"It makes me uncomfortable to see you read that magazine in my presence. Let's do this: I won't tell people your secret, and you can read it, but only when I am out of the room. Let me know when you want to read it so I can give you some privacy," Pat said. "I still want to be your friend." He held out his hand to Sean and they shook hands.

"Thank you for understanding," Sean said.

On the following Saturday, Pat and Sean walked from NSU along University Avenue to All Saints Church. They could see how well named it was, because there was a stained glass window facing the street that featured the Twelve Apostles, with each of them having tongues of fire above their heads. In addition, in every corner were statues of other saints, such as Saint Francis Xavier, Saint Thérèse of Lisieux, and Saint Anthony of Padua.

Before entering the sanctuary, they dipped their hands in the holy water and crossed themselves. They also genuflected before taking a seat in one of the pews and waited for Mass to begin. While quietly praying, their eyes roamed all around the church's interior and noticed the Fourteen Stations of the Cross adorning the walls, and the enormous altar in front of them.

When the lay reader came to the podium, the parishioners stood up. Pat and Sean joined them as the Mass began. They followed along in the Missal, and recited from memory the various passages that they knew by heart.

After receiving Holy Communion from Father O'Connell, the parish priest, they returned to their pew. Pat looked up at the choir loft and saw the stained glass window depicting the Twelve Apostles. The sunlight beaming through the glass gave the Apostles a holy look.

Before they knew it, the Mass was over. Pat and Sean walked out of the church with the other worshippers, and they shook hands with the parish priest, who was standing at the door.

While they walked to NSU, Pat said, "I could see why the church was called All Saints. Did you see all those statues?"

"My family's parish has just one statue of our patron saint, Pat," Sean said.

"My family's parish just has a stained glass image of our patron saint," Pat commented. When they reached NSU, they walked down the sidewalk to the dining hall for their evening meal before returning to their room.

On Sunday afternoon, after lunch, Pat said to Sean, "I'm going to take a little walk and get some fresh air." "Okay, Pat," Sean said as he turned on the TV set and lay on his bed.

Pat left the campus and walked down University Avenue towards All Saints Church and crossed the street to All Saints Cemetery. A wooden fence provided the border between the cemetery grounds and the sidewalk that was parallel to University Avenue. On both sides of the wide driveway, the grounds were divided into sections. Each section had a statue of a saint. Each ethnic group contained its patron saint. Saint Patrick overlooked his Irish flock; Saint Joan of Arc watched over her fellow French; Saint Anthony of Padua looked after his Italians; Saint Stanislaus Kostka was in charge of his fellow Poles; and Saint Casimir kept watch over his Lithuanian assembly. Along the driveway were the Fourteen Stations of the Cross, with the Twelth being the largest. Statues of other saints also dotted the holy ground.

Pat felt a sense of serenity when walking upon the holy ground of the cemetery. He moved about quietly and respectfully as he took in the breathtaking devotion that he felt was being emanated by the statues.

When he was finished with his tour of the cemetery, he walked back to the dormitory and joined Sean in their room.

CHAPTER THREE

It took Pat and Sean a while to become adjusted to university life: living away from their parents; having a set schedule of classes and, of course, preparations for their midterm exams. The subject of Sean's magazine was never brought up again.

In early October, Dr. Williams asked Pat to meet with her. "I would like to encourage you to apply for a position at Delacroix's Grocery Store. It's located in the Millbury Manor Shopping Center, at the corner of University Avenue and Main Street." She said when he sat down in her office. She pronounced Delacroix as "del-luh-croy."

Pat knew that Delacroix was a common French surname, and that it meant "of the cross." "Won't working there interfere with my grades?"

"Mr. Delacroix has hired many of our undergrads to work for him part-time. It would be a good work experience for you. You can work there on the weekends, so you will be able to keep on top of your studies."

"Okay, I suppose I can at least apply for a job there." Pat stood up. "Thanks for suggesting that idea to me, Liz."

"My pleasure, Pat."

Pat left her office and walked to his car. He drove from NSU and turned left onto University Avenue. He continued to the intersection with Main Street, turned right, and then turned left into the parking lot for the Millbury Manor Shopping Center. Delacroix's Grocery

Store was situated in the middle of the shopping plaza, surrounded by a variety of small stores on both sides. In addition to the specialty retail establishments, such as a bookstore, a liquor store and several restaurants, there were also a bank, a coin-operated laundry/dry cleaners, a film-processing shop and a barbershop.

Pat parked his car and entered Delacroix's Grocery Store. He stepped through the foyer and found himself facing the holiday decoration department, which was in the middle of the store. Although Christmas, Chanukah and Kwanzaa were still two months away he noticed that the merchandise for those holidays was already available for purchase. He walked down the three aisles that made up the holiday decorations department and saw a whole array of trees, ornaments, gift wrap and holiday cards on the shelves. On the other side of the aisle were shelves displaying menorahs, dreidels, and bags of chocolate candies shaped like coins. There was also gift wrap bearing designs of menorahs and dreidels, as well as greeting cards celebrating the Festival of Lights. In the next aisle were holiday decorations celebrating Kwanzaa.

After Pat walked down those aisles, he decided to tour the store, starting from the left side and working his way to the right side. He noticed that there was fresh produce as well as a floral shop. Next to that was aisle 1, which had organic and natural foods. Aisle 2 included breakfast cereals, candy and popcorn. Aisle 3 contained the canned juice as well as juice boxes. Aisle 4 had coffee, tea, crackers and peanut butter. Aisle 5 had salad dressings, ketchup, mayonnaise, and spaghetti sauce. Aisle 6 contained cake mixes, flour and spices. Aisle 7 included canned soup as well as a variety of ethnic specialties. Millbury had a sizeable population of Russian immigrants, and Mr. Delacroix was thoughtful to import food from Russia to make them feel at ease. Pat picked up a can and couldn't decipher the Cyrillic letters that were on the label. He put it back because he had no idea what it was or how to prepare it for consumption. Aisle 9 had party snacks, bottled water, soft drinks and other beverages. Aisle 10 featured the beer selection. Aisles 11 through 13 made up the holiday decorations department. Aisle 14 contained special buys, and aisles 15 through 18 were collectively known as the health and beauty shop, containing vitamins, over the counter medications, men's grooming supplies and women's makeup. Aisle 19 was the location for pet food and accessories, aisle 20 displayed household needs such as laundry soap, and aisle 21 contained paper products. Aisle 22 included commercial brands of bread, and aisles 23 and 24 were the freezer.

At the end of aisle 24, Pat came to the dairy section, where milk and orange juice were stocked. There was also a meat section along the back wall of the grocery store, as well as the deli and seafood departments. Both departments were full-service areas, so that the customers could choose to place their orders on demand. Pat continued walking past these departments, and he found himself at the starting point of his tour, the produce and flower departments.

Pat also noticed that in addition to the numerous checkout stations, Delacroix's Grocery Store also featured a customer service center, so that patrons could purchase lottery tickets and stamps and have money wired to another recipient. There was also a pharmacy located quite a distance from the customer service center. Pat decided he would like to work here. Dr. Johnson was right that working here would be a good experience for him. He asked the associate behind the customer service center if she had a blank application form for him.

"We now accept applications only by using our employment kiosk. It's on the second floor, at the top of the stairs." She pointed to a set of stairs that were to her left. "Thank you, ma'am." Pat found the staircase that the woman was referring to and climbed them. He saw the kiosk, which was situated near the employees' snack area, and sat down in front of it. He first read the introductory screen and clicked yes that he agreed to the terms, and then he proceeded to fill out the application using the keyboard. When he was finished, the system informed him that it was processing his application to see if there was a match between his skills and an open position. He continued to wait, and, in a few minutes, the system indicated that his skills met the requirements as a cashier. However, to be hired as such, Mr. Delacroix had to interview him, according to the information presented to him on the screen. Shortly after, he heard a man's voice calling his name. He stood up and said, "Yes, sir." The man held out his hand to Pat and they shook hands. "I'm Mr. Delacroix. I'd like to discuss your application with you. Please come to my office." He was wearing a navy-blue suit with a white dress shirt, a navy-blue tie, and had gray hair parted on his left side. He was slightly shorter than Pat. "I'm sorry that I'm not dressed in a suit and tie for an interview. I just planned on dropping off an application and then getting a phone call inviting me for one," Pat said as they walked down a hallway to Mr. Delacroix's office.

"That's all right, Pat," Mr. Delacroix said when he sat behind his desk in his black leather manager's chair. "Please, have a seat." He put on his half-moons and perused the printed version of Pat's application. "I see that you are an undergrad at NSU. I have hired many of your fellow students. Was that a factor in your decision to apply for a position for my store?" As Pat sat down in front of Mr. Delacroix's desk, he said, "My advisor encouraged me to apply for a position at your store, Mr. Delacroix."

"I see. What's your major?"

"Accounting, sir."

"Well, I do have an opening right now. I need a cashier. You won't be able to apply the skills that you are developing in your coursework, but at least you'll be gaining the work experience that you are no doubt trying to find. Would you be able to start this weekend? You could come here on Friday night for the new employee orientation, and then on Saturday morning you can begin your new career as a cashier. How does that sound, Pat?"

"I'll be definitely here on Friday night." "Terrific. Please get here by seven. Welcome aboard," Mr. Delacroix said as he stood up. Pat also stood up and they shook hands. "Thanks, Mr. Delacroix," Pat said before he walked down the staircase to the sales floor and through the exit doors. As he walked to his car, he could hardly wait to tell Dr. Williams the good news.

After Pat parked his car, he sprinted across the parking lot to the Administration building, bubbling over with excitement that he got the part-time job. He softly knocked on Dr. Williams' door.

Dr. Williams opened it, and when she saw his grinning face, she knew that he was successful. "Congratulations, Pat! I knew you would get the job! But I'm busy right now. Could you come back later?"

"Yes, Liz." He was so thrilled that he was successful that it didn't bother him that she was unavailable at that time to talk to him. He left her office and went to his dorm. Sean was lying on his bed watching TV. He turned it off when Pat came in. "Hey, Pat. Something new happened?"

Pat pulled out his chair from his desk and sat down. "My advisor encouraged me today to apply for a position at Delacroix's Grocery Store here in Millbury. The man who owns it hired me as a cashier. I start Friday night!"

"Good for you."

"Thanks, Sean. I'm looking forward to working there. In addition to getting hands-on experience in accounting, it will look good on my résumé."

On Friday evening, Pat went to Delacroix's Grocery Store for the orientation session, held upstairs in the snack area. Mr. Delacroix gathered his newest associates and had them seated at the tables. In front of them were their human resource folders, their nametags, navy blue jackets, and headsets. "Please fill out these forms inside your folders while I discuss my policies and procedures," Mr. Delacroix said as he perched his half-moons on the bridge of his nose. He proceeded to read aloud from his sheet his expectations from his associates, dress code, and other preliminary aspects pertaining to the business environment. The dress code consisted of a white shirt, tie and dark slacks for the male associates and for the female associates, a white blouse and either dark slacks or a skirt. The required footwear for both was dress shoes.

Then he came to the issue of the nametags, the required navy blue jackets and the headsets. "All associates must wear their nametags and their jackets. These identify you as being a member of my sales force. My radio system includes these headsets, which are used to facilitate communication among all associates. That way, my customers won't have to hear private and confidential discussions between two associates. We have a public announcement service for the needs of the customers, but when it comes to getting someone to a certain department; I would rather have that individual be discreetly summoned without our customers hearing about it."

That makes sense, Pat thought.

"This is the time clock. Everybody is assigned a random seven-digit number, which you will use to punch in at the start of your shift, to begin or end a meal period, and to punch out at the end of your shift. Everybody will also have a locker, to store your nametag, your jacket and your headset. That concludes my orientation session, folks. Any questions?"

The new associates nodded their heads that they understood his policies. Mr. Delacroix then assigned everybody their schedules, their punch numbers, and their lockers. Before leaving, everybody put their belongings into their lockers.

At six-thirty on Saturday morning, Pat woke up and took a shower. He was scheduled to work at Delacroix's Grocery Store from eight to four-thirty. After his shower, he put on a white dress shirt, navy blue tie and dark slacks. He was careful not to make a lot of noise because Sean was still sleeping. After having breakfast, he drove to Delacroix's Grocery Store. Arriving there a few minutes before eight, he waited for Mr. Delacroix to let him in. As the store owner opened the doors for him, he said, "It's nice that you are responsible enough to get here early, Pat."

"Thank you, Mr. Delacroix," Pat replied. "After you punch in, please see Scott. He will get you started on the front end."

After Pat punched in, he put on his jacket, nametag and headset. While he was sitting in the employee lounge, a man about ten years older than Pat walked over to him. "Are you Pat?"

Pat stood up and said, "Yes, that's me."

"Hello, Pat. I'm Scott. Mr. Delacroix told me that he wanted me to show you the ropes of the front end. I'm one of the front-end supervisors." He led Pat to a door and keyed a number into a panel, giving them access to half of the cash cage, which was located behind the store's courtesy counter. A wall split the room in half, with a slot emerging from it. Along this wall were three computers on a table, and in front of each computer were the chairs that the cashiers sat in to balance their drawers. "On the other side of this wall is the part of the cash cage where Darlene, one of our cash cage associates, works. She will give you your tray at the start of your shift, and after you balance it, you will give it to her."

Pat noticed that there were security cameras and mirrors everywhere. "I have to balance my own tray?" "Yes. Mr. Delacroix feels that all cashiers must be accountable for their trays."

Pat realized then that as a cashier, he would have to be careful to give the correct change to a customer. He asked, "What is the maximum tray variance allowed?"

"You cannot be over or short more than two dollars. If you exceed that variance three times in a week, you will be subject to a written reprimand." Scott gestured to a computer and Pat sat in front of it. "We are first going to have you registered as a cashier. Please find your name in the employee box."

After Pat located his name, Scott said, "You will be known as cashier 187. Enter that number in the cashier box and I will provide you with a tray." Then he went to the slot and said, "Darlene, I need a tray for Pat."

"All right, Scott." Darlene slid a tray through the slot into Scott's hands.

"At the start of your shift, you will make sure that there is exactly $200 in your tray." Scott said while handing it to Pat.

"Does it matter what combination, Scott?"

"No. But you want to make sure that you have five books of stamps." He showed them to him. They were under the twenties. Using a printing calculator, he entered 44.00. Then he counted the twenties, the tens, the fives, the ones and the rolls of coins, adding the figures on the printing calculator. "You have exactly $200, so you want to keep this receipt in your tray. Always initial and date it." Tearing off the receipt from the printing calculator, he wrote his initials and put the date on it before placing it in Pat's tray. They walked out of the cash cage.

"Welcome to the front end, Pat," Scott said. Pat stood next to him, watching the activity among the front end registers. He saw that there were lines of customers at every open register.

Scott noticed a woman quickly walking towards them. "Uh, oh.

Here comes Bernice. Come on, Pat." Scott quickly hurried over to register six. Pat followed him. Before they were able to get started, Bernice approached them.

"Scott?" she asked. "Did you get my memo to keep the conveyor belts at the cash registers always clean? We want to provide to our customers a healthy and comfortable shopping experience. As you know, Mr. Delacroix believes that a front end that looks customer-friendly *is* customer-friendly." Scott looked up, a rueful smile on his face. "I'm sorry, Bernice. I was about to show Pat here how to sign on a cash register. Today is his first day. I think I received your memo, but I must have misplaced it somehow."

"I didn't know that Mr. Delacroix hired a new cashier." Turning to Pat with a big fake smile plastered on her face, she said, "I hope you will like working here. We're like a well-oiled machine, with everybody working in harmony." Then she walked away.

"Bernice is the Front-End Manager, and my immediate supervisor. However, beneath that smiling exterior is an old-fashioned woman who feels that that only women can be cashiers. She believes that young men your age working on the front end should only be baggers and carriage retrievers. If it were up to her, you would not have been a cashier. You would have been hired just to bag the customers' orders."

"But that's discrimination." Pat said.

"And that's why she's not the store owner. She doesn't like Mr. Delacroix's hiring procedures, but as I see it, it's not for her to make decisions like that. I would recommend that you just be very careful what you say to her. Remember that memo she asked me about?"

Pat nodded. "I didn't misplace it. I put it in the circular green file."

Pat chuckled softly.

"Okay, it's funny, but we must get down to business, Pat. Let's have you sign on. Key your cashier number," Scott said, trying to regain his composure and appear professional. "Keep what I told you under your hat. You didn't hear that from me."

Pat keyed 187 and then pressed the enter key on the keyboard. Pat saw the words *Enter passcode* on the screen. 45 "That means a four-digit number that only you would know," Scott explained. Pat chose

1234, and as he keyed the numbers, a series of asterisks appeared on the screen. He pressed the enter key and the drawer opened. He placed the tray in the drawer and shut it. "Turn on your headset, put your earpiece on and switch on your light. Here is your first customer. Go!" Scott said as a woman put her selections on the conveyor belt. While he was training Pat, he also put the customers' items into plastic bags.

"Good morning, ma'am. May I have your customer card, please?"

"Yes, sir," the woman replied as she handed him her card. He scanned it and handed it back to her. Then he proceeded to scan her purchases. While he was ringing up her sale, Scott was putting the items into plastic bags. "Anything else, ma'am?"

"No, but thank you for asking," she replied.

"Your total comes to $55.75, including tax. Are you paying with cash?"

"Yes, sir." The customer took three twenties out of her wallet and handed them to him. He counted them and entered 6000 on the keyboard and then pushed the cash tender button. The drawer opened as the screen showed 4.25. Before Pat put the twenties into his tray, he pulled out four ones and a quarter. He counted them out to her, saying, "Fifty-six, fifty-seven, fifty-eight, fifty-nine and sixty. Thank you for shopping at Delacroix's Grocery Store. Have a good day."

"You're welcome," the customer said as she placed her bags into her shopping carriage.

Then the next customer in line handed Pat his customer card, and another sale was being processed. The man was paying with a check. "Scott, how do I handle this check?" he asked.

"We now process checks electronically."

"The customer wants thirty dollars cash back."

"Yes, that's okay, because the store policy allows checks to be accepted no more than thirty dollars over the total." Scott directed him to key 7437 on the keyboard and the pressed the check tender button. A response came on the monitor, signaling that an authorization was in progress. After the check was approved by the system, a message appeared on the display indicating that the check needed to be voided. After Pat voided the check, a slip was printed out for the customer to sign. After the customer signed it, Pat put it in the appropriate slot and handed the man the check, a twenty-dollar bill and a ten-dollar bill out of his drawer when it opened. He said, "Twenty and thirty. Thank you for shopping at Delacroix's Grocery Store this morning, sir. Have a good day."

While working at the cash register, Pat listened to such announcements over his headset as, "Dave, please help the customer with the Red Sox baseball cap in the meat department."

Besides cash and checks, Pat learned how to process credit card payments, debit card transactions with cash back to a customer, bottle refunds, manufacturers' coupons, and electronic benefit payments. Before he knew it, his shift was up, and Scott reached over to shut his light off. "Now I am going to show you how to balance your tray."

Pat signed off his register and the drawer opened. Pat took his tray out, making sure that he had all the different forms of tender in it. He followed Scott to the cash office. He sat in front of the computer workstation. After he located the record of his tray in the computer, he started balancing it by counting the money in it and entered that figure. Then he also counted the numbers and amounts of the other forms of tender and entered those figures in the appropriate places in the electronic worksheet. Then he had the computer balance his tray. It was over by a dime in cash. He printed out the report.

"Very good for your first day, Pat," Scott said he handed him two plastic bags. "These are your drop bags. After you balance your tray and print out the report, you must leave in $200 for your next shift. Using the printing calculator, you will determine how many of each denomination you will set aside. The rest of the money will go into these drop bags. The manufacturers' coupons, bottle refunds, checks, and credit card drafts go into your brown envelope." He handed him one that had slots for the different forms of tender. "Put your number on it." Pat wrote his cashier number on the brown envelope. Then he counted out $200 in a variety of coins and bills. After he did that, he tore off the slip of paper from the adding machine and put that in his tray, with his initials and the date. He noticed that on the bags were two columns: one for the number of bills and coins and the other for the amount. He put the extra bills in one bag, added up the total and sealed the bag, noting the drop bag number on his report. Then he completed the same procedure for the surplus coins. Then he slid his tray, his report, his bags, and the brown envelope through the opening.

"Thanks, Pat," Darlene said when she accepted everything. "I'll tell Mr. Delacroix that you are doing a fine job," Scott said as he held open the door for him. "See you next week."

"Thanks, Scott," Pat said before he punched out at the end of his shift. He went to his locker, removed his nametag and his headset and put them away. Taking off his jacket, he folded it over his arm and went to his car.

Pat returned to his dorm, where Sean was studying at his desk. He looked up when he saw Pat come in. "Ready to go to church this afternoon, Pat?" Sean looked at the clock. It was quarter to five.

"Sure. Let me get changed first and we can leave at ten minutes past five." He removed his dress shirt and slacks and put on a plaid shirt and blue jeans.

Then the two roommates went to All Saints Church and then went to the dining hall for their supper.

"How was your first day of working at Delacroix's Grocery Store, Pat?" Sean asked after they sat down at a table in the dining hall. Pat replied, "I'm a cashier. We must wear headsets and balance our own drawers."

"Was it busy?"

"Constantly. It was non-stop action. All I did was slave over a hot cash register, Sean."

"But it's good work experience. You'll be hired as a full-time employee after graduation and be set for life. You can work for Mr. Delacroix in the accounting department."

"That might be a possibility. I could advance up the corporate ladder because I'll have the education as a qualification," Pat said as they finished eating. They brought their trays to the staff attendant supervising the dining area. They left the dining hall and went to their room.

During the two next months, Pat and Sean went to their classes, studied and took their tests. They related well to each other and with the rest of the other students in their classes. Pat also managed to keep his grades up while working at Delacroix's Grocery Store. Liz was especially glad that he was doing very well. Sean was also relieved that Pat respected his privacy regarding the magazine.

At the end of the fall semester, NSU was closed for the holiday break, which began the Friday before Christmas and continued to the Monday after New Year's Day. After their classes were over, Pat and Sean were in their room, packing to go to their homes.

"I got you a little gift, Pat," Sean said as he handed his roommate a plastic bag. "It's a little token of appreciation for understanding."

Pat opened the bag and took out a wall calendar featuring wildlife scenes. "That's very nice of you, Sean. I got you something also." He gave Sean a plastic bag.

Sean opened it up and took out a calendar that had photographs of Irish landmarks, such as the Blarney Castle. "Thank you, Pat."

When they finished packing, they locked their door and went to their cars in the parking lot. "See you next year, Sean," Pat said as he opened the passenger side of his car and put his suitcase on the seat.

"Okay, Pat," Sean said as he watched his roommate drive out of the parking lot. Then he sat behind the steering wheel of his car and drove home.

Pat could hardly wait to tell his parents about living on campus and about his part time job at Delacroix's. When he came home, his father held open the screen door as Pat brought his suitcase inside. "Welcome home, Pat," his father said.

"Hello, Mom and Dad." Pat sat in one of the recliners in the living room.

"Anything new?" his mother asked.

"Yes. I have a part-time job at Mr. Delacroix's Grocery Store."

"Whose idea was that?" his father asked.

"My advisor. She said that many NSU students work there. I'm a cashier. We must wear headsets and balance our own trays."

"Sounds like good work experience," his father remarked.

"That's what Sean said."

"Who's Sean?" his mother asked.

"Sean Donnelly is my roommate. He's also of Irish descent, and he lives down in Winston," Pat said. "Our Christmas break ends the Monday after New Year's Day, so I will leave on Sunday. I also don't have to work during the break at the grocery store, since Mr. Delacroix doesn't expect me to drive back and forth from his store. Then after graduation, he will promote me to his accounting department."

"My son, I am so proud of you! I knew that being an accounting major would lead to realistic employment," his father said. "Everything is working out the way it should."

CHAPTER FOUR

On the Sunday after New Year's Day, Pat and Sean once more found themselves in their dorm. "Did you have a good Christmas?" Sean asked Pat as they unpacked.

"My father was especially proud that I am working at Delacroix's. He's hoping that Mr. Delacroix will hire me on a full-time basis in accounting and make practical use of my education."

The spring semester started the Monday after New Year's Day, and Sean decided that in the afternoons while Pat was working at Delacroix's, he would try to get his body into shape. After his classes were over for the day, he went to the gymnasium and inquired about using the weight-training room. He approached the staff member supervising the participants. "I'd like to start working out, sir."

"Absolutely, young man. I'll have Joe show you around." The staff member shouted, "Joe! Please come over here."

Joe came over to them, and Sean noticed that his hair was matted to his forehead. "Yes, Steve?"

"Joe, meet… I'm sorry; I didn't get your name," Steve said to Sean.

"Sean Donnelly."

"Joe, please show Sean our facility." Sean and Joe walked around the gymnasium, as Joe explained the machines and the muscle groups that were targeted. "What muscles are you looking to improve, Sean?"

"I'd like to have bigger biceps."

"We can start you off with lifting weights, Sean," Joe said. "Let me go to my dorm and get a T-shirt, gym shorts and a towel, so we can get started," Sean said.

"No problem, Sean," Joe said. Sean eagerly walked to his dorm and located a clean T-shirt, a pair of gym shorts and a towel. He put them inside a gym bag. He also had a padlock, which he put in his gym bag. Then he returned to the gym for his workout. He changed in the dressing room before entering the gym.

"Ready, Sean?" Joe said when he saw Sean entering the gym.

"Yes, I am, Joe."

"We're going to have you start with something light, and then work your way to heavier weights. Lie on your back, and I'll spot you." Joe handed Sean a ten-pound barbell. "Lift up and down the barbell ten times. Each time is called a rep. It's short for the word repetition." After Sean completed that exercise, Joe said, "Let's try the twenty-pound barbell. Do ten reps."

Sean spent the next hour with Joe using the barbells. As he was working out, he felt the issues in his mind dissipate. A sense of serenity came over him. An hour passed and Sean was surprised that the time flew by. He felt his skin was all sweaty, and he rubbed his face with his towel. "I need to take a shower now, Joe. Thanks for spotting me today. I'll probably come back next week." He grabbed his towel and went to the dressing room.

Standing in front of his locker, Sean pulled off his shirt and gym shorts and stuffed them into his bag. He noticed that the other guys in the dressing room were nude and unashamed about their bodies. Feeling just as confident, he stripped off his boxers and put them in his locker before shutting the door. He threw his towel over a shoulder and went to the showers.

Standing under one of the showerheads, he relaxed away the tension he felt building up in his muscles. He also listened to the idle chatter that the other weightlifters were engaged in. He also casually glanced at their physical attributes. It occurred to him that since he and the other guys were nude, the playing field was level and there was no chance to feel that he was inferior. He had just as much right to be working out as they did. He realized that looking at them without their clothes on was a lot better than the photos of the models portrayed in the magazine. But he was careful not to stare at them.

Sean noticed that the guy across the shower from him looked a lot like the centerfold in his magazine: thick black hair and mustache, a very hairy chest and his groin was lily-white, in stark contrast to the rest of his tanned body. The guy turned around and Sean couldn't take his eyes off the perfectly formed back. His buttocks were also not tanned. Then he quickly averted his eyes as the guy turned around to face him, because he didn't want the guy to think that he was gay.

After his shower, he went to his locker and changed into his clothes before returning to his dorm. He looked at his watch and saw that it was almost five in the afternoon. The sun was beginning to set, and he decided to go to his dorm to relax for a while before dinner. Pat was still working at the grocery store, so he had the room to himself. After he put away his gym clothes, he lay on his bed and closed his eyes. Images of the other guys in the showers filled his mind, as he contemplated their physiques from head to toe. He fell asleep shortly after, with a smile on his lips.

Sean awoke with a start when he felt that the sun had disappeared from his window. It was completely pitch black as he sat up and yawned. Rubbing his eyes, he got up from his bed. His stomach was rumbling, and he realized that he was hungry. He decided to go to the dining hall for supper.

It was strange eating by dinner by himself, Sean realized, as he went through the serving line, choosing what to eat and where to sit. Usually, he and Pat sat together. Since his roommate was working at the grocery store, Sean knew that he would have no company for dinner. However, as Sean was making his way to find an empty table to sit, he heard his name called. He looked around for the direction of the voice that calling him. "Over here, Sean."

Sean focused on the guy calling him. He didn't recognize who was addressing him. "How do you know me?" he asked.

"I'm Joe. I spotted you in the gym this afternoon. Sit down with my friends and me."

"Now I remember who you are! I'm sorry, Joe, I was so excited about working out that I forgot that I met you today." Sean put his tray on the table and pulled out a chair. He sat down.

"Sean, I'd like you to meet my friends. This is Todd, Ben, and Jeremy. Guys, this is Sean Donnelly. I was spotting him in the gym."

"I saw you in the showers today, Sean," Todd said. "You did?" Sean asked. "I stood in front of you. You don't recognize me with my clothes on."

Sean suddenly looked at Todd's face and recognized the black mustache perched above his mouth. "I hope you didn't think I was staring at you." Todd laughed a little. "I'm proud of my body, and I'm glad that other people appreciate the hard work that it takes me to look like this!"

Ben asked Sean, "Where are you from?" "I'm from Winston, in the southern part of Connecticut."

"What's your major?"

"Mathematics." Sean started eating his dinner.

"How do you like living on campus, Sean?" Jeremy asked.

"It's okay. My roommate, Pat, and I get along well with each other." "Where is he?" Joe asked. "He's a cashier at Delacroix's Grocery Store here in Millbury. He's hoping to get practical, hands-on experience for his degree in accounting." Sean felt himself relaxing, glad that he was able to talk to these guys as if he was their friend. While they were engaging in casual conversation, he forgot all about his secret magazine. After dinner, they stood up from the table and brought their trays to the staff member. "I had a good time meeting all of you, guys," Sean said as they walked out of the dining hall.

"We did too, Sean," Joe said. "I'll probably come back for more weight training next week, around three in the afternoon on next Monday, Joe. It was nice meeting you and your friends. Goodbye." Sean walked to his dorm.

"See you them, Sean," Joe said as he and his friends walked to their dorm.

When Sean reached his dorm, he lay on his bed and closed his eyes. He was glad that he was making friends at college and that no one suspected that he had homosexual inclinations. He really didn't feel that way towards other men, but he was concerned that someone might get that idea about him.

While these thoughts were going through his head, he heard the door open. Sitting up on his bed, he rubbed his eyes while adjusting to the overhead light being switched on.

"Sorry, Sean," Pat said as he pulled out his chair and sat at his desk. "It's okay, Pat. How was work?"

"Busy. It was customer after customer during my shift. I really enjoy applying the accounting concepts that I learn in the classroom to real-life situations. It's really providing me with actual work experience," Pat said as he opened a textbook and started doing his homework for a class he had in the morning.

"I went to the gym today, and I met some nice guys there, who want to help me build my body," Sean said.

Pat looked up from his textbook. "Did you have a nice time, Sean?" "Yes. I enjoyed working out with them." Sean lay down on top of his bed. "I'll be quiet, so you can study without being disturbed."

"Thanks, Sean. I really appreciate that." Sean then closed his eyes and he fell asleep in a few minutes. He dreamed about working out with the guys in the gym. Images of him showering with them filled his mind while he slept.

Around ten that night, Sean suddenly awoke at the sound of Pat getting out of his chair. "What time is it, Pat?"

Pat looked at his watch. "It's a few minutes past ten. I'm going to get ready for bed, Sean." He changed into his pajamas.

"I didn't know I was going to sleep for such a long time! I thought I was going to take a nap." He yawned and stretched his arms. Getting up from his bed, he undressed to his boxer shorts before pulling back the bedspread, the blanket and the sheet and sliding under them. He pulled them over him and rested his head on his pillow. "Good night, Pat," he said as he closed his eyes. "Good night, Sean," Pat said as he switched off the overhead light and got into his bed.

The next morning Pat and Sean went to the dining hall for breakfast. After they received their meals and holding their trays, they looked for a table to sit. Sean heard his name called. "Sean, sit with us!" Joe was waving his hand.

"Hey, Joe!" Sean said enthusiastically as he walked over to Joe's table. He saw that Todd, Ben and Jeremy were sitting there also. "Can you make room for my friend Pat?"

"Of course, Sean!" Todd said. Pat and Sean sat down at the table between Joe and Todd. "Guys, this is Pat, my roommate," Sean said.

"Nice to meet you guys," Pat said as he shook hands with each of them. "Sean told me that he met you in the gym. You're his workout buddies."

"Sean told us that you're an accounting major, and that you have a part-time job as a cashier," Todd said. "Right. It's my goal after graduation to use my education and experience in a well-paying job and be set for life."

"Where did you get an idea like that, Pat?" Joe asked. "From my father. I really wanted to be an English major since I enjoy writing. But my father believes that writers are strictly freelance, and that the income is only sporadic. He didn't want me to be singing for my supper. Since he's paying for my college tuition, I must do what he says."

"Doesn't he know that the English majors don't always end up as freelance writers? There are other opportunities such as teachers or journalists," Ben asked.

"His mind is made up, so he wouldn't consider any other viewpoint. Besides, I have faith that my education will not go to waste," Pat said. After breakfast was over, they went to their morning classes. Pat and Sean each concentrated on their coursework before getting together for lunch. Then they went to their afternoon classes.

After his last class that day, Pat went to work at Delacroix's Grocery Store. He prepared himself for another thrilling day as a cashier by getting a till from the cash office and plugging his headset into his ear to listen to broadcasts from the other associates. It was repetitive: greeting a customer by saying hello; asking for the customer's loyalty card; processing the order; accepting the payment from the customer and thanking the customer for shopping at Delacroix's. The cycle never once deviated from this pattern. Although Pat did most of the speaking, his voice never showed any sense of exhaustion. Then it was time for Pat to close his register and balance his till at the end of his shift. He realized that he really enjoyed working at the grocery store. He felt that he was able to apply his accounting coursework to the real world. This thought came to him as he drove to his dorm.

While Pat was working at Delacroix's, Sean went to the gym to exercise. He found that building up his body was a great way to release the tension that was building inside. As he walked inside, Joe saw him. "Hey, Sean, come over here to my friends and me. You remember Todd, Ben and Jeremy."

"Hey, guys," Sean said. "How are you doing?"

"We're just getting started, Sean," Todd said. He was lying on a mat face up, his hands gripped around a barbell. "Watch me doing ten reps."

"That's nothing, Todd," Ben said. "I can do twenty."

Todd got up and let Ben take his place on the mat. After Ben finished his reps, he said, "Sean, let's have you do twenty."

Sean lay on the mat and Ben carefully handed him the barbell. Sean was able to do ten reps before putting it down on the floor. "That's enough for me, guys," he said weakly because he was out of breath. He lifted the bottom of his tee shirt and brought it to his face, mopping the sweat with it.

While Sean was catching his breath, he watched the others pumping iron. After they were done, Sean said, "Let me try again." He lay on the mat and Todd spotted him. He was able to do twenty reps before stopping. "I think I'll take a shower," he said as he stood up. Going to his locker, he removed his sweaty tee shirt and shorts, putting them inside the compartment, and threw a towel around his neck. Before entering the shower area, he slid off his underpants and hung them on the hook and placed his towel over them. He stepped into the shower area and turned on one of the showerheads. As he stood under the spray, he felt the water was relaxing him.

Todd entered the shower area and turned on a showerhead. Standing in front of Sean, he said, "Sean, I'm glad that you and I are friends. I feel I can trust you. You don't seem to be judgmental."

"What do you mean, Todd?" "I'm going to let you in on a secret." Todd looked around to see if anyone else was in the shower area. He wanted no one else to hear what he was going to tell Sean. "I like to work out because it gives me a chance to look at other guys without their clothes on."

"I have a confession to make, Todd," Sean said quietly. "I like to look at naked guys also."

"So we have something in common."

"Yes, but let's keep it to ourselves. I almost got in trouble last fall because Pat discovered my magazine." "I know what you mean. I also have bought that magazine in the past." Todd said as he and Sean left the showers. They went to their lockers and changed into their clothes.

CHAPTER FIVE

The Hibernian Brothers spent the next three years at NSU studying for their college degrees: attending classes, studying and taking tests. Pat also continued working at Mr. Delacroix's Grocery Store and Sean was diligent in maintaining his body.

Upon his impending graduation, Pat approached Mr. Delacroix one day. The store owner was in his office, sitting at his desk with his half-moons perched on his nose, hunched over paperwork. Pat knocked on the open door.

"Please come in, Pat," Mr. Delacroix said as he looked at Pat over his half-moons. "Have a seat. What can I do for you today?" Pat sat down in front of Mr. Delacroix's desk. He took a deep breath before speaking. "Next month I will be graduating from NSU with a degree in accounting. Is there any chance that you would consider me for a position that would make use of my education?"

"I would like to employ you full-time. There is a position that I want you to assume." Pat looked at Mr. Delacroix eagerly. "Will the position make use of my accounting knowledge? Will the pay be commensurate with my education?" A wide smile crossed his face, anticipating good news.

Mr. Delacroix looked sternly at him. "First of all, I don't pay higher wages to an associate just because that individual has more education. I also don't move people up my company ladder just for that reason. To reduce competition among my associates, if someone in a higher-paying capacity leaves my store, I hire an outside candidate who may have the right experience for the vacancy being created, rather than offer a promotion to a current associate. In your case, if you want to be a full-time associate, it won't be on the front end, because I only hire part-time cashiers. You will also find that employers don't use education as the sole criterion to determine career advancement. For your information, years of service doesn't necessarily guarantee a higher job classification. I know that philosophy is contradictory to what you have learned at NSU. I have a business to run, and your instructors were so busy being professional scholars that they have no grasp of the real world. It's too bad that you were under the impression that having a college degree would mean more money, but you must remember that your professors were only interested in keeping their jobs. They are very isolated from the real world because they are living in the ivory towers of academia."

"So where would you assign me?" Pat asked.

"The only position I have that has a vacancy is in the Celebrations department. You'll be working for my Celebrations manager. He will schedule you as he sees fit, and you will do what he says. If he says, 'Jump!' your only response will be, 'How high?'"

"How much would you pay me per hour, Mr. Delacroix?"

Before responding, Mr. Delacroix opened a database file in his notebook computer, which contained the salary information regarding his employees. "Currently you are earning $14.25 an hour. By transferring you into that full-time position, I will pay you an extra dime per hour. I don't provide a differential compensation for working on Sundays. The position that I am assigning you to has a maximum pay rate of ten dollars an hour. Unfortunately, I can't pay you that wage just yet. You would have to work productively to receive that wage. Based on your annual reviews, I will keep giving you raises based on merit until you are 'maxed out.' Once that happens, then I will give you longevity raises at a dime per year."

Pat took out his calculator from his pocket and used it to determine his yearly salary. "Forty hours per week at $14.35 an hour is $574 a week.

Four times $574 is $2296 a month. Twelve times $2296 is $27,552 a year, before taxes. That's way below average for a college graduate. My father will not be happy when he hears this, Mr. Delacroix." Pat turned off his calculator and put it back in his pocket.

Mr. Delacroix's face suddenly turned the color of vine ripened tomatoes as he said, "It is not your father's right to tell me how much money I should pay you. The labor market is in favor of the employers such as me. You really can't expect to get paid more money for having a college degree. If you were to work anywhere else, you would make not much more than minimum wage. I'm doing you a favor by keeping you employed here. At least you have a job. Besides, this yearly wage that you have calculated is above the poverty level. You will not be destitute. You are earning above the minimum wage."

"So, you're saying that I'm lucky to have a job here, Mr. Delacroix? What will my parents think?"

"As the store owner, I have the right to do what I please with my associates. I really don't care what your parents think. They do not have the right to tell me how to do my job. Just so you know this, you will be expected to be available to work every day from eight in the morning to eleven at night. Keep in mind that you will have two weeks of vacation and four personal days per year. Mr. Harris will provide you with the time off at his discretion. You will also work three of the six holidays per year, at time and a half. He will decide which of those days he will need you. Like all my full-time associates, you are required to be available to work every hour of every day of every month of every year for as long as you are an associate. That means you will have a rotating schedule according to my staffing needs. Don't try to predict how you will be scheduled because there will be no rhyme or reason. Moreover," he continued, "I expect that for you, working here will be your sole priority. I don't allow my associates to work anywhere else. If you don't think that the salary that I will be paying you is sufficient, that's your problem, not mine. If you find that you are having a hard time making ends meet, then it's your responsibility to correct that, without having to take on a second job. I absolutely forbid that. You would have to make sacrifices in that event to balance your budget. You might need to cut back on some luxuries. Am I making myself clear?"

"Yes, sir," Pat said dejectedly. Mr. Delacroix's face returned to its normal pale color after he finished speaking. "When do you graduate? I need to know so that Mr. Harris can put you on his schedule."

"I am graduating two weeks from Friday, Mr. Delacroix."

"Good. Then you can start the following Sunday at eight in the morning. On that day, we will make up your schedule for the rest of the week." Mr. Delacroix nodded slightly, indicating the conversation was over. "Good. Then you can start the following Sunday at eight in the morning. On that day, we will make up your schedule for the rest of the week." Mr. Delacroix nodded slightly, indicating the conversation was over. Mr. Delacroix thought to himself, Pat *doesn't know that I am assigning that position because he is single and doesn't have a family.*

Pat left Mr. Delacroix's office, disappointed that he couldn't apply his education to get a higher-paying position. However, that feeling paled to the disappointment of his father. He drove home to tell his parents his news. "Mr. Delacroix is going to transfer me from the front end to the celebrations department."

His father asked, "The celebrations department? What does that mean?"

"I will be working in that department, Dad." "How much will you be earning an hour?"

"Fourteen and thirty-five cents an hour, Dad."

"Only $14.35?" "And I would have to work on Sundays."

"I hope you would get time and a half for working on Sundays." "No. Mr. Delacroix doesn't pay time and a half for working on Sundays."

"But what about your accounting degree, Pat?" his mother asked. "We put you through college so that you would learn something practical, have job security, and be set for life."

"You better buckle down and get going with your career search. No way is any son of mine going to let his university degree go to waste by letting an employer walk over him," his father interjected. "And you should stay away from those get-rich-quick pyramid scams. They are nothing but con artists, unscrupulous snake-oil salesmen trying to swindle hardworking people out of their money. The only people who make money in those rip-offs are the ones who prey on those naïve to fall for such ruses. It might seem to be a business opportunity, but I wouldn't consider it. If you must spend money to make money in such a situation, then there's something wrong with it. Remember, there's no such thing as a free lunch. If someone tries to give you something for nothing, there must be a catch. Don't just walk, run away! Also, don't allow yourself to be in a position where you try to give something free, because nobody will want it. As my father used to say, 'a fool and his money are soon parted.'"

"I know better than to spend money to make money. It's just that right now working at Delacroix's is the only employment opportunity. So, while I am working full-time, I could still send out my résumés to accounting firms in the meantime. At least it's steady work, because I know that other people in my class have no employment prospects whatsoever. Don't worry; everything will turn out right, Mom and Dad."

"I hope so, for your sake," his mother replied. The big day of graduation was finally here, thought Pat as he and his parents were driving to NSU for the graduation ceremony. He was dressed in a suit and tie. He and the other graduates were also wearing caps and gowns. All the graduates and their guests filled the enormous auditorium, where the graduation ceremony was held. They were quietly talking to themselves while waiting for it to begin.

A hush overcame the assembly as the university president began the graduation ceremony by giving a speech. Pat, his fellow graduates, their parents, and other guests listened intently to his speech. After he finished speaking, he was followed by other speakers, including the salutatorian and the valedictorian. After the end of the last speech, each graduate was presented with his or her degree from the respective dean.

Pat's parents took a picture of him receiving his bachelor's degree from the dean of the school of business studies, attesting that he met the university requirements for his major in accounting.

Sean's parents also photographed their son receiving his bachelor's degree in mathematics from the dean of the school of arts and sciences.

After the graduation ceremony, Pat made his way to Sean and his parents. They shook hands upon greeting one another. "This is my former roommate Pat, Mom and Dad."

"It's a pleasure to meet you, Pat," Mr. Donnelly said.

Sean asked Pat, "Where are you going to work?"

"I'm going to stay at Mr. Delacroix's store at least until the end of summer, while I apply for positions with accounting firms, Sean. He's going to put me in the celebrations department. How about you?"

"I've been hired as a full-time teller at a local bank in my hometown. It's strictly entry-level, but it's a start." Then Sean realized that Pat was alluding to the fact that having a bachelor's degree wasn't necessarily a ticket to advancement up the corporate ladder. "Mr. Delacroix isn't going to promote you up to a higher-paying position? I thought he would, since you have a degree in accounting," Sean said.

Pat said, "It just so happens that he thinks a university education isn't a qualification for an automatic promotion."

Sean asked, "What do your parents think?"

"They don't like it, but at least I have a job. I know many other people who are graduating, and they must send out résumés and have interviews. They have no job prospects lined up. At least I have one." Pat saw his parents walking towards him. "Mom and Dad, this is my roommate, Sean Donnelly."

"Nice to meet you, Mr. and Mrs. Kavanaugh," Sean said as he shook hands with Pat's parents. "During the summer, we can get together. I would like to stay in touch with you, Sean," Pat said. "I would like to do that." Sean pulled out a business card that featured his contact information. "I had these cards professionally printed." He gave one to Pat.

Pat looked at it before putting it in his wallet. "I am very impressed with it, Sean." "I think it's time to leave, Pat," Sean said as he shook hands with his former roommate. "I'm looking forward to staying in touch with you." Then he and his parents left the auditorium. Pat saw Liz walking towards him. "Hello, Pat. I'm glad that you are now a graduate of NSU. Are these your parents?"

"Yes, Liz, they are."

"I'm Dr. Elizabeth Johnson, Pat's advisor," she said as she shook hands with his parents. "You must be so proud of your son, Mr. and Mrs. Kavanaugh!"

"We're glad that he received his degree in accounting, but we're disappointed in that he's not able to apply himself in that line of work, Doctor," Mr. Kavanaugh announced.

"What do you mean, sir?" she asked.

"We just found out that Mr. Delacroix, the owner of the store where Pat has been working while attending classes at NSU, will not promote him to his accounting department," Mrs. Kavanaugh declared.

"I'm not able to get involved in human resource issues. I told Pat that Mr. Delacroix hires undergraduate students to work for him at his store, to get work experience, but it's up to Mr. Delacroix to proceed as he sees fit, and I have no authority. At least Pat has a job. It's a tough labor market right now, so Pat's lucky in that respect. There are hundreds of other graduates who don't have prospects. It was nice meeting you," she said. "Good luck, Pat." Then she walked away.

Pat and his parents walked out of the auditorium to their car for the ride home. Pat's father gripped the steering wheel as he drove. "How dare she encourage our son to work at Delacroix's, when Mr. Delacroix won't advance Pat up his corporate ladder! Whatever happened to applying yourself by showing some initiative? That's what my father would have believed in."

Pat said, "Unfortunately, times are different now, Dad. It's not her fault. That's just how it goes. She thought it would be a good place to get work experience," Pat said. "I still plan to send out résumés during the summer."

"We spent thousands of dollars on your education, so you would be set for life. Why can't Mr. Delacroix accommodate you?" Mr. Kavanaugh asked.

"Well, Dad, he's not under any obligation to place me in a higher-paying position." Pat said.

His father looked in the rearview mirror to see Pat. "I'm really disappointed with you!" "Me? What did I do?" Pat asked.

"You're letting Mr. Delacroix walk all over you like a doormat. Show some backbone and force him to give you a job that pays more."

John Kavanaugh's voice rose in pitch; his words were angrily ripped from his throat.

"You're being unreasonable. I can't do that," Pat said meekly. "You can't afford to work there. You must look for another job." His father thundered the words.

"I have all this summer to apply for positions that are advertised. Don't worry because I will find something." He hoped his father would find those words to be reassuring.

"All this yelling is giving me a headache, guys," Maureen Kavanaugh spoke up. She was relieved when her husband pulled into the driveway of their home. "Let's give the situation a rest."

Because Pat had to go to work at eight at Delacroix's on Sunday morning, he went to the Vigil Mass on Saturday afternoon at his home parish, Saint John the Evangelist. While waiting for the Mass to begin, he prayed quietly that he would find a job that would make more use of his accounting degree. While kneeling in prayer, his mind was filled with apprehension. He felt torn between two opposing viewpoints: his parents versus Mr. Delacroix, and he was caught in the middle. He wasn't sure who had the upper hand in this dilemma. He decided the only way to go was to take it one day at a time.

After the Mass was over, he drove home to have dinner with his parents. While they were eating, his father said, "Tomorrow you have to go to work at eight in the morning, right, Pat?"

Pat nodded. "Yes." Pat's bedside alarm went off early Sunday morning, and he got out of bed. He first took a shower before getting dressed. He put on a white dress shirt, dark slacks and a solid navy-blue tie. Then he went to the kitchen for breakfast. His father was sitting at the kitchen table, drinking a cup of coffee. "I see you are ready to go to work, Pat." Pat nodded.

"Yes, Dad. I'm going to the store after I eat." He opened a cabinet and put a box of cereal on the kitchen counter. Locating a cereal bowl, he poured the cereal into it and brought it and a spoon to the table. Then he put two drinking glasses on the counter and filled them with milk and orange juice. Bringing those to the table, he set them next to the cereal bowl and the spoon before sitting down. Then he sat at the table across from his father and started eating.

"I realize that I might be coming across to you as angry, but I only want the best for you, my only son," Pat's father said.

"Yes, Dad. I understand." "Why can't you go to Mr. Delacroix and tell him that you have a university education, and to have him put you in a position that makes use of it?"

"Dad, I've tried. His mind is made up and he doesn't want to budge. It's beyond my control." Pat finished eating and stood up. "I'm going to the store now. See you in the afternoon." Then he went to his car and drove to Delacroix's Grocery Store.

When Pat came to the store, Mr. Harris greeted him. He was taller than Mr. Delacroix, with black hair, a pair of thick, black-rimmed glasses covering dark brown eyes and a full black beard. He was wearing a white shirt open at the top, with his necktie loose around the collar. "We open the store at nine on Sundays, Pat. Welcome to my department." He held out his hand to Pat. "After you punch in, I will give you a list of tasks for you to work on."

"Thank you, Mr. Harris," Pat said before going to the time clock. After he put on his nametag, jacket and headset, he found Mr. Harris by the courtesy counter. "Here is a copy of the sales flyer, Pat. Please also put up the sales signs in front of the ad merchandise that's located in the celebrations department." Mr. Harris said as he placed a sales flyer and a stack of sales signs on the counter in front of Pat.

Pat looked at the merchandise featured on the sales flyer that was in the celebrations department. As this was the week before Memorial Day, which traditionally marked the beginning of summer at Delacroix's, the merchandise was geared towards summer entertaining and lawn care. Holding them in his hands, Pat went to the celebrations department and quickly wasted no time by placing the sale sign by the grass seed bags that were on the shelves. He also found the gas grills and their accessories and put the sale signs in front of them. He used scotch tape that he found in a filing cabinet in Mr. Delacroix's office.

Pat was almost done when Mr. Harris came over to him and said, "That's done incorrectly, Pat." The celebrations manager had finished putting his tie around his collar and was wearing his suit jacket, with his nametag in place. Pat was surprised to say the least.

"What's wrong with the way I was putting them up? You said to place the signs in front of the ad merchandise."

"But you were supposed to put them in the plastic sales sign holders that we use. I thought you knew that."

"No. I wasn't aware of that, sir." "Well, you are going to have to do this over, and this time, do it right. We've already wasted half an hour of Mr. Delacroix's time. His motto is that if you are going to do something, do it right or don't do it at all. He allows very little room for employees' mistakes. How long have you worked here?"

Pat felt embarrassed but understood Mr. Harris' point of view, although he seemed to come across as unusually harsh. "Since I was a first-year student at NSU, Mr. Harris. Where do I get the sign holders?" "We have them in the filing cabinet located in Mr. Delacroix's office, Pat. Please get enough of them, as we can't waste any more time by making more than one trip. It's already twenty minutes to nine. The customers will be coming to shop." Mr. Harris glanced impatiently at his watch.

Pat walked to Mr. Delacroix's office and found the plastic sign holders in the bottom drawer of the filing cabinet. Racing back to the celebrations department, he quickly put the sale signs correctly. Just as he was finishing the task, he heard Mr. Harris' voice over the store's radio system. "Good morning, all Delacroix's Grocery Store associates. We are open for business. Have a good day." After a pause, Mr. Harris announced, "Pat, please come to the service counter." Pat walked to the service counter, where he saw Mr. Harris waiting for him.

"Yes, Mr. Harris."

Mr. Harris said, "I'm sorry that I snapped at you earlier this morning. I was under the impression that you knew what was expected of you."

"It's okay, sir," Pat replied. "What I would like you to do is for me at this point is just help the customers in the celebrations department. You don't have to worry about stocking shelves or ringing a register. Just straighten the shelves when you're not with a customer in the meantime."

"Okay, Mr. Harris." Pat spent all that Sunday morning and afternoon just making sure that every customer who needed assistance was taken care of. He answered any questions that they had for him. When he didn't have any customers who needed his help, he went down the aisles of nine through eleven and brought all the merchandise to the front of the shelves. Then at five o'clock, he took off his nametag, jacket and headset, put them in his locker, and punched out to go home. During supper that night, his father asked, "Pat, how was work today?"

"It seems I can't do anything right!" Pat exploded, tears running down his face. "What happened, honey?" his mother asked. "My first day of work as a full-time employee, and already I feel like giving up."

"What do you mean?" his father asked. "Mr. Harris, my boss, asked me to put up the sale signs in the celebrations department before the store opened this morning. I thought I was putting the sale signs correctly. Then he came over and told me that I was putting them the wrong way. If that weren't enough, he made it sound as if I didn't know what I was doing. The implication was that it's stuff I should know by now."

"That's business for you. They want you to be efficient and productive. I was hoping that Mr. Delacroix was going to put you to work in his accounting department," Pat's father said.

"But, Dad, that's beating a dead horse. He's never going to give me that kind of work."

"Do you want me to talk to him, Pat?"

"The last thing that Pat needs is for you to get involved for him, John," Mrs. Kavanaugh spoke up. "Just leave things be. He needs to stand on his own two feet. He must have a sense of independence."

"But I can't sit by and let my only son get beaten by the system. What's this world coming to if people are just going to sit back and let bosses tell them how much money they are allowed to earn? Whatever happened to 'an honest day's pay for an honest day's work?' Those were the words of my father."

"Times have changed, Dad," Pat said. "It's all about holding down costs, including overhead. Besides, isn't it a little presumptuous on my part to think that Mr. Delacroix is going to put me in a higher-level position and pay me accordingly, on the virtue of having a college degree?"

"But we put you through four years at the university to ensure that you would be rewarded handsomely," Mr. Kavanaugh replied.

"Dad, it's beyond my control. What would you like me to do: argue with Mr. Delacroix? Tell him that I deserve more money? It just doesn't work that way."

"Then you better get your act together this summer and look for a job that pays more money!" As Mr. Kavanaugh shouted, a vein in his neck suddenly bulged.

"All right, John. I think he's gotten the message." The cool, reassuring voice of Maureen Kavanaugh cut through the air, breaking the tension between father and son.

After dinner was over, Pat said, "I'm going to my room to apply for jobs." He went into the living room to get the employment section of the *Mid-Connecticut River Valley Sunday News* and then went to his bedroom with it. He had his laptop and his all-in-one peripheral on his desk. Pat focused on the positions that were entry-level and only required a bachelor's degree. He knew that he had no hands-on experience and therefore couldn't apply for one that mandated years of practice as a qualification. He found three available jobs that were looking for entry level accountants. Bringing the employment section to his room, he turned on his computer and loaded Microsoft Word. Having created his résumé during a required career-planning course, he retrieved it from the documents folder of his computer. He printed out three copies of it. After his all-in-one peripheral finished the print job, he found himself confronted by the white screen of a new Microsoft Word document. A scary thought came to mind. He had no idea what to write! Panic settled in. Then he remembered a book that he had bought at the campus bookstore that concentrated on employment searches. He used an example in the book as a model for designing a cover letter. It specified the margins on top and bottom as well as the sides. He set up the margins accordingly. Using the model found in the book, he wrote the cover letter:

64 Middle Road
Newcastle, CT 06—
(860) 555-2233
PKavanaugh1@galaxy.net
June 30, 2022

Ms. Heather Gamble,
Associate Director of Human Resources
Corning/Lowell & Company
1500 Main Street Mapleton,
CT 06—

Dear Ms. Gamble:

I am applying for the position of junior accountant that was advertised in yesterday's edition of the *Mid-Connecticut River Valley Sunday News*.

I have a bachelor's degree in accounting from Nutmeg State University, having recently graduated last month. My GPA was 3.37.

I have been working at Delacroix's Grocery Store in Millbury for the last four years while I was pursuing my undergraduate degree.

Enclosed is my résumé. References are available upon request. I look forward to meeting with you to discuss my qualifications and experience, as I feel that my skills are a good match for the needs of your organization. I will give you a phone call as a means of gauging your interest in my application for this position.

Sincerely,

Patrick J. Kavanaugh

After proofreading the cover letter, he printed a copy. Making changes in the destination address and the salutation, he created two more cover letters and printed them. He saved all three documents in a folder on his desktop.

Using labels, he printed one for his return address. Then he copied the destination address from the cover letter and pasted that onto a second label. He followed the same procedure for the other two cover letters before handwriting his signature in the space between the word "Sincerely," and his printed name. After carefully folding the cover letter and the résumé into thirds, he put them in the envelopes and licked the seals.

By the time he was finished, it was nine in the evening, and Pat decided it was time to go to bed. He had to be at work at Delacroix's at eight in the morning.

On his way to work the following Monday morning, Pat stopped at the post office to buy three stamps and mailed his résumés and cover letters to the firms. He hoped that his applications would have a successful employment outcome on a financial basis.

Pat suddenly realized while working one day that there were four female associates who weren't required to work flexible hours; they were scheduled only mornings and afternoons. While on his afternoon break in the associate lounge, he asked Jim, an associate who worked in the deli department, about them. "I noticed that there are four women who seem to only work until three in the afternoon."

Jim replied, "They are UPC administrators. Their job is to maintain shelf-edge item integrity. If there is a price change, they must update the sticker in front of the items on the shelf to minimize scanning inaccuracies at the checkout."

"I had no idea that such a position in the store existed. Mr. Delacroix told me that all full-time associates must be available to work mornings, afternoons and evenings. Why is that they can have a set schedule and go home at three in the afternoon?"

"Well, Pat, they can have the luxury of having so-called 'mother's hours' because they have children and have to be home for them."

At this point Mr. Harris came into the associate lounge. He'd overheard the discussion between Pat and Jim about other associates' schedules. "Pat, I'd like to talk to you privately." He escorted Pat into the manager's office. Mr. Delacroix was sitting at his desk, filling out paperwork. Mr. Harris closed the door behind him and directed Pat to have a seat.

"I overheard Pat asking questions about the availability of other associates, Mr. Delacroix." Mr. Harris fixed Pat with a stern look on his face.

As with discussing hourly wages among my staff, I don't tolerate my associates questioning how other associates are being scheduled, Pat," Mr. Delacroix said quietly. He was angry that Pat was taking it upon himself to get involved in other associates' schedules.

"I think it's a double standard that I have to be available for work every hour of every day, for your convenience, while they can work a fixed schedule."

"Again, that's my concern, not yours. End of discussion. You are free to go back to work, Pat," Mr. Delacroix declared.

Chastened, with his facing burning hot with embarrassment at being scolded, Pat left Mr. Delacroix's office and went to the general merchandise department to finish his shift. He began hoping that his career would turn around in such a way that he could leave Delacroix's in style and substance.

CHAPTER SIX

While Pat was working at Delacroix's on a Monday afternoon, his cell phone received an e-mail message. He read it during his lunch break. Ms. Gamble from Corning/Lowell & Company was interested in having him come in for an interview. He quietly but enthusiastically called the number provided in the e-mail message, because he didn't want anyone in the break room to overhear his conversation and possibly report his activity to Mr. Delacroix.

"Hello, this is Pat Kavanaugh. I would like to speak to Ms. Gamble, please."

"This is Ms. Gamble, Mr. Kavanaugh. How are you, sir?" A woman's pleasant voice replied. Her tone was in marked contrast to Mr. Delacroix's abrupt nature.

"I'm fine, ma'am. And you?"

"I'm doing splendid. Thanks for asking. We received your application, and I would like you to come in sometime this week. What day is good for you?"

Pat walked over to the bulletin board while holding his cell phone to his ear to check his schedule for that week. He was off Wednesday and Thursday. "I could come in either this coming Wednesday or Thursday. I'm off those two days this week."

"We look forward to meeting you on Wednesday at 9:00 a.m. Do you need directions?"

"No, Ms. Gamble." Pat had researched the company's location using the Internet and had directions printed out in advance.

"All right. When you come to the reception area, tell the receptionist that you have an appointment with Human Resources. I'll be waiting for you. Any questions?"

"No, but thank you for asking."

"Goodbye, Mr. Kavanaugh," Ms. Gamble said before she hung up the telephone.

Pat was so excited about the prospect of having a real fulltime job that would have, in his opinion, a higher entry-level wage, and a regular schedule that would entitle him to be off nights, weekends, and holidays. He felt he deserved such bonuses because he had a bachelor's degree. He was subscribing to the belief that a college graduate should be guaranteed a higher-paying salary than one who only was a high school graduate. He spent the rest of the day at work feeling that he might be able to break free from the tyranny that Mr. Delacroix held over him.

On Tuesday night, before Pat's interview, he called his friend Sean to tell him the latest news about his job search. "I hope that I can escape from Delacroix's, and if I get this position, Sean, my father will be pleased with me."

"What's going on with Delacroix's, Pat?"

"I'm caught between my father and Mr. Delacroix. I thought that having a college degree would elevate me to a higher-paying position, and I'm disappointed that it didn't work out that way. Unfortunately, my father is very upset. He thinks that I am allowing myself to be a doormat. Even though my heart was set on being a liberal arts major, it didn't seem to be able to provide for long-term job stability. My parents felt that having an accounting degree would guarantee that I would be set for life."

"Well, you know what they say: father knows best. I know that you must work every Sunday. Do you get time-and-a half?"

"No, I don't."

"I suppose your father is pretty upset with you." "Dad thinks that I have no backbone; he says that I am allowing Mr. Delacroix to walk over me."

"Did you explain to him that it's a tough labor market?"

"Dad doesn't care about that. He clings to expressions from my grandfather's work experience."

"It sounds like you're caught between the proverbial rock and a hard place. Neither side will budge." "My father's angry with Mr. Delacroix. He wants to give him a piece of his mind. I'm caught between my parents and Mr. Delacroix. I feel as if I am being pulled in two different directions. My parents want me to succeed, but I don't think that's possible because Mr. Delacroix is adamant that he's not going to promote me just because I have a college degree. My father would really like to go to him and force him to give me a high-paying position, but I know that's not how it works."

"I don't know what to tell you, Pat."

"Mr. Delacroix told me that I would have to be available to work every day from eight in the morning until eleven in the evening. That was to his expectation for me because I am a full-time associate. Then I discovered that there were four full-time associates, all women, who had so-called 'mother's hours' and were not required to work an unpredictable schedule. I felt a double standard was in practice and I said so. Boy, did I get into hot water for that!"

"So tell me about this position." "It's a firm called Corning/Lowell & Company. They were looking for an entry-level accountant. I have an interview tomorrow at their offices. They're located in Mapleton. I mailed them my résumé and a cover letter, and yesterday I received a response through my e-mail account. I called during my break and scheduled an interview with them on Wednesday. What's going on with you, Sean?"

"I am a teller at Winston Savings Bank. It's a position that I can do in my sleep. Once I got the hang of deposit and withdrawal procedures, it became second nature for me. I am on my feet all day behind the counter. The bank is in the downtown section of Winston, across from the Town Hall. I also rent an apartment that's within walking distance from the bank."

"What does your apartment look like?" "It's in a building called Winston Arms Village. It consists of three wings in a semi rectangle: the left and right wings face each other, and the center wing faces Main Street. There are two floors, with the second floor accessible by three stairways from the first floor. There are railings along the edge of the concrete sidewalk. It almost looks like a motel. My apartment has two bedrooms, a living room, a small kitchen, a bathroom, and two closets. The one window looks out onto Main Street."

"I would like to see it sometime, Sean."

"You can come down here on your day off. I must hang up now. It was nice talking to you. Good luck with your interview, Pat. Goodbye."

"Goodbye, Sean."

On Wednesday morning, Pat put on his business suit, consisting of a navy blue pair of slacks and a matching suit jacket. He wore a white dress shirt with a solid blue necktie. He wanted to look as professional as possible. After getting dressed, he went to the living room where his mother was watching her daily morning television program. "Mom, I have an interview today in Mapleton." Maureen Kavanaugh looked up from the TV set. "Good luck, dear." She quickly stood up to give him a hug and a kiss. "I hope you get the position. Your father will be so proud of you!"

"Thanks, Mom," Pat said as he left the house and went to his car. He opened the driver's side and placed the copy of directions he had printed from his computer on the passenger's seat. After getting buckled in, he started driving to Mapleton. He arrived at the parking lot fifteen minutes earlier than his scheduled interview for Corning/Lowell & Company. He parked in one of the spots reserved for visitors and went to the front door of the building. Pat approached the receptionist's desk and introduced himself to the young man sitting behind the counter. "I have an appointment with Ms. Gamble, sir."

"Please fill out these forms, and I'll let Ms. Gamble know you are here," the young man replied. He picked up the receiver and dialed Ms. Gamble's number. "Hello, Ms. Gamble. Mr. Kavanaugh is here. Thank you." Turning to Pat, he said, "Ms. Gamble will be with you momentarily. Please wait for her, sir."

"Thank you, sir," Pat said as he took the forms that were attached to the clipboard and sat in a chair in the waiting room. He filled them out, answering such questions as who should be called in case of an emergency, his work availability, and his desired salary range. When he was done, he placed the clipboard on the chair next to him and waited for Ms. Gamble. When Pat saw a well-dressed woman with well-coifed blond hair and a few strands of pearls around her neck, he stood up to greet her.

"Mr. Kavanaugh?" she asked. "I'm Heather Gamble." She held out her hand to him.

"Yes, Ms. Gamble. Pleased to meet you," Pat said as he shook hands with her.

"Please come to my office so we can discuss the position." Ms. Gamble led him down a hallway and to an office on the right. "Please take a seat, Mr. Kavanaugh." She nodded towards the chair in front of her desk, as she closed the door. Ever the gentleman, he waited for her to take her seat before sitting down in his. "I must say that I am very impressed by your résumé. You certainly have a solid work ethic. Let me tell you about our company and the position we are looking to fi ll." She described in detail the responsibilities of the job and the expectations required of the successful candidate. Pat listened to her speak, nodding to acknowledge his comprehension of what she was saying. After she finished, she asked, "I'd like to hear about a typical workday at Delacroix's. What do you do there?"

"I work in the celebrations department. It's my duty to display the seasonal merchandise. I also must maintain the appearance of the shelves."

"Tell me about your studies at Nutmeg State University."

"To get a bachelor's degree in accounting from NSU, half of the required 200 credits were in required courses in accounting and general business principles and the other half were required courses in a variety of the arts and sciences."

"Do you have any questions for me, Mr. Kavanaugh?" "No, ma'am, I don't." She got out of her chair and opened the door of her office. "I'll walk you to the reception area." When they reached the reception area, she held out her hand to him and they shook hands. "I'll be in touch with you, Mr. Kavanaugh. Take care."

"Thank you, Ms. Gamble." Then Pat walked out of the building to his car in the parking lot.

CHAPTER SEVEN

While Pat drove to work to Delacroix's the day after the interview, his thoughts were focused on his responses to Ms. Gamble concerning his experience. He hoped he made a good impression on her. He desired a favorable outcome so that the chips would fall into place and his hard work applying himself in his university studies would ultimately lead him into a promised land of sorts.

Mr. Harris was waiting for him by the time clock. "Pat, after you punch in, I have a list of things for you to do." He handed him a slip of paper.

Pat read the list. Number One, as always, was take care of the customer!!! The other items were arranged in the order of importance. Since the Fourth of July holiday was over the past week, the next holiday to plan for was Labor Day. The shelves in the celebrations department were empty, waiting to be filled.

An assortment of end-of-summer items, such as holiday themed paper plates and napkins, bags of plastic forks, knives and spoons, and other picnic supplies were in the cartons. There were also garden and lawn care items. They were stacked one on top of another on a pallet in the celebrations department.

Before stocking the shelves, Pat placed the preprinted labels in the grooves that Mr. Harris generated from the store's main computer. Then he stocked the shelves with the merchandise in the cartons.

After he stocked the merchandise according to the layout plan created by Mr. Harris, he priced the items, making sure that the price tags were in the upper right corner of each package. The final touch was straightening the items on the shelves to produce a look of uniformity. Not only would be pleasing to the eyes of the customers, but more importantly, it would show to Mr. Delacroix that he was productive. Also, he hoped to inspire the store owner to make an exception and promote him up the corporate ladder if his job search was not to his advantage.

That was not the case for Pat that day. Mr. Harris, always eagle-eyed and obsessively focused on the minutest detail, happened to notice that Pat made one little mistake: the grooves were a little sticky from past labels. Standing very close to the counter, he pushed his glasses on top of his head and squinted at the grooves. "You forgot to clean these grooves before placing the labels on them, Pat." He put his glasses back on his face. "If you're going to do something, do it right the first time. Besides, you should know to do these things without having to be told. This is a definite lack of productivity."

Pat felt himself getting red in the face, so embarrassed he thought he was going to cry. Keeping his composure, he said, "I thought I was doing my best, Mr. Harris."

"Well, you're not. Clearly you are not cut out for this type of work. So, either you shape up or you ship out! And you won't find another employer that is going to pay you the salary you are getting from Mr. Delacroix. Our customers are expecting more from us, so you will have to start managing your time more effectively. You are wasting Mr. Delacroix's time and money. And for your information, if you were to work anyplace else, you would have to start off at minimum wage, so I would recommend that you buckle down. You need to work smarter and be more productive if you want to stay employed here. We know that you have a bachelor's degree, but that doesn't mean you should expect to be compensated for having one. It doesn't award you a higher-paying salary."

"I can always transfer back to the front end, Mr. Harris."

"Unfortunately, I won't allow you to transfer. Mr. Delacroix needs you to work for me. So, for along as you work at this store, I will always be your boss. This discussion is over, Pat."

At that moment, Pat realized he had to get another job as soon as possible. An inner voice told him that he was too smart for this place, and he realized he had to leave Delacroix's – the sooner the better. The writing on the wall was becoming very apparent. He kept having a nagging question in his mind: "What did I do wrong?" He was under the impression that if he worked hard enough, he would advance to a higher-paying position at Delacroix's. The proverb he operated under, which he learned from his father, was that willingness to work hard guaranteed advancement up the corporate ladder. He concluded that working hard didn't carry as much weight as working smart. He spent the rest of his shift working on the other tasks Mr. Harris had assigned him, all the while watching the clock until it was time to punch out and go home.

While he was forming these opinions in his mind, he was startled to hear his name being paged on his headset through the store's radio system. "Pat Kavanaugh, please report to the front end of the store. Code PC." Pat temporarily stopped the project he was working on and headed to the checkout area of the store. A Code PC meant that there was a question about a price check. The always prominent Bernice approached him with an item. "Pat, this bag of charcoal didn't scan a price. It wasn't in the store's master item file. Could you get a price for it right away?"

"Yes, Bernice, I'll get you a price for it. I'll announce it on my headset." Pat quickly went to the area where the bags of charcoal were located and found the one that the customer was wanting to purchase. Using his headset, he paged over the store's radio, "It's $2.49, Bernice." Then he returned to his project.

When Mr. Harris came over to see how he was progressing, Pat said, "There was a Code PC on a bag of charcoal. You can show me how to add the item to the store's master item file, Mr. Harris?" "That really isn't something I can demonstrate to you. Besides, it will be in the computer with Karen tomorrow."

"What does that mean?"

"It's just not for you to know how to do that. For the record, I'll have a lot of work to do tomorrow. Karen, one of our UPC administrators, will take care of it for me then. Don't concern yourself with such trivial matters, Pat. It really isn't that important." In other words, *it's none of my business. I'm not allowed to learn anything else that might upset the delicate associate balance in this store that is known as the status quo*, Pat thought to himself after Mr. Harris walked away. He shook his head as he watched Mr. Harris' figure become smaller and smaller until he disappeared. Finally quitting time at five arrived! Pat punched out and headed to his car. As he drove to his house, he hoped that sometime soon a new career opportunity would be waiting for him.

While having dinner with his parents, Pat discussed the experience he had with Mr. Harris. "It's as if they think they are doing me a favor by keeping me employed. Mr. Harris must enjoy reminding me that he is my boss."

"I think you should look elsewhere, Pat," his father commented.

"I have been applying for positions, and I had an interview this week. But Mr. Harris told me that I can't expect to start at a higher than minimum wage per hour with any other employer. It seems as if he has a hand wrapped around my neck. He even said to me that he will always be my boss if I work at Delacroix's, Dad."

"Your father and I have been talking about how you demonstrated such independence from us when you lived at the university," his mother announced. "We would like to help you move into your own apartment. We can provide a security deposit for you. All you would have to do is pay rent and manage your own monthly expenses."

"I would like to first see if I can get a job with Corning/ Lowell & Company."

"Well, you can still look for an apartment, while you waiting to hear from them," his mother said.

After dinner was over, Pat made a phone call to Sean to tell him what was going the latest news. "Sean, this is Pat. How are you doing?"

Sean answered, "I'm still at the bank. How is your job search coming along, Pat?"

"I had an interview last week. I'm waiting to hear from them. But I have the pressure to find another job as soon as possible. I really can't take much more frustration at Delacroix's."

"What happened?"

"I can't do anything right! It was my responsibility to set up a new display for end-of-summer items. I thought I was doing my best! Mr. Harris told me that I failed to follow through by not cleaning the grooves where the labels are placed. One little mistake, and he chided me for it. Then he gave me the impression that they were doing me a favor by keeping me employed, when the labor market is teeming with more qualified applicants than I am and that I would start at minimum wage anyplace else. So, it's his way or the highway!" Pat sighed heavily. Sean replied, "Nobody said it was going to be easy." "I suppose so. I was wondering if I could come down tomorrow to visit you at your apartment." Sean smiled at the prospect of seeing Pat again. "It would be nice to have you over on Saturday. How about lunch at noon, and then we can catch up on old times." "I would like to have lunch with you then. Could you give me directions?" Sean said, "You take the Constitution State Turnpike south to exit 18. You turn right onto Main Street, and you go through five stoplights. At the sixth stoplight, you turn right into the parking lot for my apartment complex. I'll meet you in the parking lot."

"Thanks, Sean," Pat said before hanging up the phone.

On Friday Pat went to work at Delacroix's. Mr. Harris scheduled him to work the afternoon shift, from 12:30 until the store closed at 9:30. As usual, his boss was waiting for him by the time clock, a look of anticipation on his face. "Why do you always meet me here, Mr. Harris?" Pat said as he punched in and put on his jacket. "That's part of being your supervisor, Pat." Mr. Harris involuntarily smoothed down his necktie. Pat had been noticing that every time Mr. Harris expressed the phrase "that's part of being your supervisor" he put his hand on his necktie. It was as if the gesture always accompanied the phrase. "You must really enjoy saying that. I've lost count the number of times you have repeated that phrase."

"Now, Pat, try to understand. You work for me for as long as you are employed here. Here is your list of things to work on tonight, after I leave at five this afternoon." Mr. Harris handed Pat the piece of paper. "Try to get as much done as possible."

"Mr. Harris, I have a doctor's appointment next week. It's on Thursday. Do you suppose you can schedule me the entire day off?"

"Yes, I can do that. But just remember that if I need a day off you will have to accommodate me by working that day for me. It goes both ways. You know you must be available to work every hour of every day of every week of every month of every year for as long as you are employed here. I shouldn't have to make schedule changes for you. That's Mr. Delacroix's policy." Pat said to himself, *I don't get it. One day he is asserting his dominance over me by reminding me that he is my boss, and then turns around and says stuff like that.* He realized that some questions are better left unanswered. This quandary had all the markings of an enigma. "I also was wondering if I could be scheduled next Tuesday from seven to four, Mr. Harris," Pat asked.

"If I were to comply with your request, Pat, Mr. Delacroix would wonder why you would be in so early on that day."

"So? He can always ask me." Pat was bemused at how rigid and inflexible Mr. Harris was behaving. It made working at Delacroix's more difficult. Pat felt as if his needs were in direct conflict with the needs of Mr. Delacroix, and the potential for a dangerous situation was imminent. At five that afternoon, Mr. Harris went to see how much Pat had accomplished. He was stocking the shelves with picnic supplies: plastic bottles for condiments; packages of paper plates and napkins; and bags of charcoal. "Keep up the good work, Pat. You are making progress. I will see you on Monday. Have a good day off tomorrow." He walked through the front doors of the store, leaving Pat alone to finish the items on the list. At the end of his shift Pat went home. On Saturday morning Pat had breakfast with his parents. "Today I am going to have lunch with Sean. He invited me to his apartment in Winston." "It looks like it's going to be a nice day for a drive, son," his father said. "Have a good time, dear," his mother said. Pat put his cell phone in his pocket before getting behind the steering wheel of his car. After putting on his sunglasses, he started his car and followed the directions Sean had given him. As he drove south along the Constitution State Turnpike, he saw the exit for Nutmeg State University. A sense of nostalgia came over him. Suddenly he recalled the first moment when he met Sean, and he was grateful that they were still friends after all these years. Pat saw that he was approaching exit 18. He slowed down so he could get onto the ramp that would bring him to Main Street. At the end of the road he turned right. As he drove on Main Street, he counted the five stoplights as he went through them. At the sixth stoplight, he turned right and drove into the parking lot for the Winston Arms Village. As he parked his car in the parking lot, Sean, who was watching for him from his apartment, walked to Pat's car. "I'm glad that you were able to come this afternoon, Pat." He threw his arms around Pat. "I have lunch ready. Then after we eat, I'll take you on a little tour and then we can catch up on what's been happening." Pat followed Sean to his apartment. Sean opened the door for Pat and they walked inside. Sean walked through the living room towards the kitchen, which was at the opposite end of the apartment. A window looked out on the grounds behind the apartment building. On the stove was a pot of tomato soup and in the oven were freshly melted cheese sandwiches. Sean had already set the dining table with bowls, plates, silverware, glasses and napkins. "Take a seat, Pat." Sean pulled out a chair from the table. Sean then ladled the soup into the bowls before placing the pot on the stove. Then he opened the oven and removed the sandwiches from it. He placed one on each plate. After filling the glasses with water, he opened a box of snack crackers and took out one of the sleeves and opened it also. "Help yourself to as much as you would like, Pat," Sean said as they sat down. Pat sat across the table from Sean. He dipped the spoon into the thick tomato soup and brought it to his lips. He let the silky liquid slide onto his tongue and down his throat. Then he took a bite of the grilled cheese sandwich; it was a tasty accompaniment to the velvety texture of the soup. "This is very delicious, Sean," Pat said before biting into a cracker. "This would be a nice lunch to have on a rainy day. You are such a talented cook." "This is the kind of lunch my mother made for my father and me on Saturday afternoons," Sean said as he dipped his cracker into his soup, letting it get covered by the red liquid before eating it. After lunch was over, Pat helped Sean clear the table by removing the dishes, silverware, and glasses and placing them in the sink. Sean turned on the hot water, and Pat squirted dishwashing liquid into the sink. They worked together, washing not just the plates and eating utensils, but also the pots and pans. After drying everything, Sean put the dishes and other utensils back into the kitchen cabinets. Then he took a washcloth and cleaned the crumbs off the dining table, carefully catching them into his hand. Walking over to the cabinet under the kitchen sink, he opened the door and dumped the crumbs into the wastebasket. Then he unplugged the kitchen sink and let the dishwater empty through the drain. The last thing he did was to rinse the remaining soap suds from the sink. "Ready for a tour of my apartment, Pat?" Sean asked as they walked into the living room. "You've already seen my kitchen and living room." Sean opened the door to his bedroom, and they walked inside. Sean's neatly-made bed was next to the wall. A bureau was on the opposite side of the bedroom. A bedside table with two drawers had an alarm clock on top. A window also afforded a view of the front parking lot. "I also have a walk-in closet and a bathroom," Sean said as he opened the closet door and they walked in. "And there's the bathroom." He pointed to it at the end of the closet. "You have quite a place," Pat said. As they walked out of Sean's bedroom, Sean pointed to the room opposite his bedroom and said, "That's the second bedroom for guests." "Wow, Sean. I'm impressed that you have a lot of room in your apartment," Pat said. "Thanks. Let's go into the living room and watch a movie," Sean said as they walked out of his bedroom. Going to the DVD cabinet, Sean picked out a film. "How about this movie?" He held the DVD so Pat could see the title. "Sure." Pat sat down in the armchair positioned near the kitchen while Sean put the DVD in the player. Then Sean sat down in the couch located against the wall of the living room. He switched on the TV set and in a few moments the DVD began playing on the screen. During the next two hours, while watching the movie, Pat totally forgot about what was bothering him regarding his job search. He was so absorbed with the movie's characters and plot. He realized that no matter what would happen to him, Sean would be there for him, through thick and thin. After the movie was over, Pat said, "I think it's time that I better get going, Sean." "Thanks for coming over and visiting with me, Pat. I'm glad that we're still friends." Sean threw his arms around Pat in a bearlike hug. Then Pat walked out of Sean's apartment and to his car. When Pat came home, his mother handed him a thin envelope. It bore the logo of Corning/Lowell & Company. He knew instinctively, without having to open it, that the letter inside wasn't good news. He slid open the seal of the envelope and read the enclosed letter:

Corning/Lowell & Company
an accounting firm
1500 Main Street
Mapleton, CT 06—

Mr. Patrick Kavanaugh
64 Middle Road Newcastle,
CT 06—
July 25, 2022

Dear Mr. Kavanaugh:

Thank you for your interest in our firm. I regret to inform you that in our candidate search for the position of junior accountant, we have selected another individual whose qualifications better match our requirements for the vacancy. Please be advised that we will keep your résumé on file for one year, if a position that requires your unique set of skills becomes vacant. It was a pleasure to have met you and we wish you the best of luck in your career search.

Sincerely,

Heather P. Gamble

Maureen Kavanaugh saw the disappointment in her son's eyes. "They didn't hire you for the position that you wanted? I'm sorry about that. But it's all going to work out. Just keep having hope. After dinner, your father and I have something to discuss with you." Pat nodded as he put the letter and envelope into the paper shredder and turned it on. A sense of finality came over him as he watched the pieces of paper become garbage. "How was your visit with Sean this afternoon?" Pat smiled as he told his mother about it. "Sean made tomato soup with grilled cheese sandwiches and crackers. Then we watched a DVD. It was good to see him again."

CHAPTER EIGHT

While Pat and his parents were eating dinner that night, Pat's mother said, "I was really impressed that your friend Sean moved into his own apartment. We think it's time that you did the same." "But I still am looking for a job that pays more than what I get at Delacroix's. I really don't have enough money saved up for a security deposit," Pat replied. His father said, "Don't worry about that. We will help you with the security deposit. You will only be responsible for the monthly rent." "I guess it is time for me to spread my wings and live independently," Pat said. The next day after work Pat searched through the advertisements in the *Mid-Connecticut River Valley Sunday News* for apartments available for rent. He found a few vacancies that interested him. One was in Mapleton, another was in Newcastle, and a third was in Millbury. He circled the ads in the newspaper and decided that he was going to call the numbers listed and make appointments to see them. Pat first called the number of the apartment in Mapleton and arranged with the owner, Mr. Thompson, to look at it after work on Wednesday afternoon that week. After leaving Delacroix's on Wednesday afternoon, Pat drove to the address in Mapleton given to him by Mr. Thompson, who also provided him with directions from Millbury when Pat mentioned that he worked at Delacroix's. He parked his car by the side of the house, which was in a rather rural part of the town. The house looked to be about a hundred years old. Mr. Thompson was waiting for him at the front porch. "Pat?" "I'm Pat, sir." "I'm pleased to meet you. I'm Henry Thompson." The man with salt-and-pepper hair was about ten years older than Pat's father was. Black-horned rims were perched on his nose. They shook hands. Then Mr. Thompson unlocked the front door and they stepped inside. "You will be renting one of the rooms upstairs. You will also share the kitchen, living room and the upstairs bathroom. I have two other tenants who live here, both young guys like you." Mr. Thompson led him up the staircase to show him the room. Opening one of the doors, Mr. Thompson escorted him inside. The room had three windows: one looked out into the side yard and the other two looked over the road. "Now let me show you the rest of the house, Pat." Mr. Thompson said as he led him out of the room and shut the door. Pat noticed that the other bedroom door was closed. He realized that one of the other tenants rented out the bedroom. "Here's the bathroom." Pat walked inside and stood by the window, which looked out over the backyard. Pat looked at the toilet and the sink and pushed aside the shower curtain to see the bathtub. Then he walked out of the bathroom. "Let me show you the downstairs areas." Mr. Thompson walked down the staircase, with Pat behind him. They came into the living room, which had two chairs and a couch, and a TV set mounted on the wall. There was another bedroom next to the living room. "This is Bob's room. He has been here the longest. John is the other roommate that lives upstairs. They're not home right now." They came into the kitchen, which had a table and chairs, cabinets, a refrigerator, sink, and a range. Various appliances also dotted the countertops: a toaster, a microwave oven, a coffeemaker, and a blender. "The monthly rent for the room is $400 a month. I will also need two months' rent in advance as a security deposit," Mr. Thompson said as he pulled out a chair at the kitchen table and sat down. He nodded to Pat to do the same. "Also, you will be expected to share in the costs of the utilities: heat, electricity, cable TV, and telephone. You will keep your room neat and shovel the driveway and sidewalks with your housemates when it snows. You will help maintain the house's appearance, both inside and outside. Do you have any questions, Pat?" "I don't think so, sir. Let me think about this for a while." "For your information, I have other applicants who are looking to rent the room. Time is of the essence if you want to live here, Pat," Mr. Thompson said as he and Pat got up from the kitchen table. "Thanks for letting me see the room, Mr. Thompson," Pat said as they shook hands and then he walked to his car. When Pat came home from looking at the house, he discussed the terms of living as a tenant of Mr. Thompson with his parents. They agreed that he should accept the offer. "I think this is a good opportunity for you to live on your own. We will take care of the security deposit for you. Call Mr. Thompson and tell him you will take the room," his father said. Pat dialed Mr. Thompson's number on his cell phone. "Mr. Thompson?" "Yes, it is. Is this Pat?" "Yes." "I'm sorry, but I just rented the room to another guy." "Oh, I see. Thank you anyway. Goodbye." Pat disconnected the call on his cell phone. A look of disappointment came over his face. "What happened, Pat?" his mother asked. "He already found another tenant for the room." Pat opened the *Mid-Connecticut River Valley Sunday News*. Having previously selected other ads in the paper, he called the number of the apartment that was for rent in Newcastle on his cell phone. "I'm interested in the apartment that was advertised in the *Mid-Connecticut River Valley Sunday News,* ma'am," he said when a woman answered his call. "I live in Newcastle." "You can come over and look at it right now. What's your name, please?" "I'm Pat Kavanaugh, ma'am." "I'm Mrs. Hollister, Pat. Please come to 62 Elm Street. Do you know where that is?" Pat recognized the street name. He remembered that it was a side street off Main Street in the downtown part of Newcastle. "Yes, Mrs. Hollister, I know how to get to Elm Street." "I will see you shortly. Goodbye, Pat," Mrs. Hollister said. Turning to his parents, Pat said, "I'm going to look at another apartment right now. It is here in Newcastle. See you in a half hour." Pat left his house and walked to his car. He started it and drove to Mrs. Hollister's house. He had no problem locating it: a two-story saltbox house situated in a residential neighborhood. It was painted sky blue with emerald green shutters. He parked his car on the street and walked to the front porch. As he opened the screen door to knock on the heavy wooden door, a woman in her early fifties with graying blond hair opened it and gestured for him to step inside. "I'm Mrs. Hollister, Pat. Welcome to my house." She offered her hand to him. "And this is my husband, Tom," she introduced him to a man standing in the hallway. Like his wife, Tom was also in his early fifties. His thick beard was silver in some spots. "It's nice to meet you, Pat," he said as he shook hands with him. "Hello, Mr. and Mrs. Hollister. Thank you for giving me a tour of your apartment."

"It's a spare room that we are looking to rent out. It's upstairs." Mrs. Hollister led the way through the living room to the second floor, climbing an intricately designed staircase, with a solid oak banister. As they walked into the hallway at the top of the stairs, she said, "There are three bedrooms: my husband and I have the master bedroom in the middle, and our eighteen-year-old son has the room on the far left. The room we are looking to rent is on the far right." She walked to a door and opened it. All three of them stepped inside. A hardwood floor and flat white paint were the only things in the room. Two windows looked out into the street. "Let's talk about an agreement, Pat," Mrs. Hollister said. She waited until he stepped into the hallway and then she shut the door. While they were walking down the staircase, she said, "As a renter, you will have kitchen privileges. You will have to wait until I am through cooking before you prepare your meals. You will also clean up after yourself. I would suggest having your own silverware, cookware, dishes, and glasses." "Do you require a security deposit? What would the monthly rent be, Mrs. Hollister?" Pat asked as they came into the kitchen. Mrs. Hollister pulled out a chair at the kitchen table and sat in it. Mr. Hollister sat across the table from her. He nodded to Pat to sit at the table with them. "The rent would be $400 a month, and I would need two months' rent as a security deposit," she said. "Plus you would contribute to the household utility bills, Pat," Mr. Hollister announced. "Also, you would help me around the house, such as mowing the lawn, shoveling the snow and other tasks." "Let me think about it, Mr. Hollister," Pat said as he shook hands with both of them. "Thank you for giving me a tour of your house," he said as Mrs. Hollister opened the screen door for him and he stepped out into the driveway. He walked to his car and drove back to his house. The next day, on his way to work, Pat saw a house that had a sign on the front lawn indicating that there was a vacancy. The house was located about three blocks away from the Millbury Manor Shopping Center, on University Avenue. Pat thought that he could live in the house and then walk to work, rather than driving a car. He could save on gas in the end. He pulled over to the side of the street and wrote down the telephone number posted on the sign. Then he continued driving to the store. Pat called the number on his cell phone while on his break. A man's voice came on the other end. "Hello." "Hello. This is Pat Kavanaugh. I work at Delacroix's Grocery Store in Millbury and I saw that you have an apartment to rent in a house on University Avenue. I would be interested in looking at it." "I'm the owner of the house, but I don't live in it. The apartment is the entire first floor. I have tenants on the second and third floors." "I'd like to come over this evening after I get off work at five." "Yes, you could see it then. I'm Steve Mulligan, Pat." "Okay, I'll see you then. Goodbye." "Goodbye, Pat." Pat suddenly realized that he should give Mrs. Hollister a call to let her know that he was not interested in renting a room from her. He dialed her number on his cell phone. He recognized her voice when she answered his call. "Hello?" "Hello, Mrs. Hollister. This is Pat Kavanaugh." "Hello, Pat. Unfortunately, we found another individual to rent the room from us. Thanks for calling." "Well, I was calling to let you know that I wasn't going to rent the room. Therefore, it all works out for the best for all of us. Goodbye, Mrs. Hollister." "Goodbye, Pat." Mrs. Hollister hung up the telephone. Pat put his cell phone into his pocket and went back to work. After Pat punched out at the end of his shift at Delacroix's, he drove to the house on University Avenue. As he parked his car, he saw the shadow of a man inside the open front door. The man exited the house as Pat was walking up the driveway. "Pat, I'm Steve. Let me show you the first floor." They shook hands before Steve opened the screen door to let Pat enter the foyer. A stairway to the second and third floors was on the left side of the entrance hall. Steve unlocked the heavy wooden door to the right of the hallway and opened it. "This is the apartment that I am looking to rent out." He led Pat on a tour: living room, eat-in kitchen, bedroom, and a bathroom. There were also three closets. Two front windows looked out into the front of the house, and there was a window at the back of the house. "The rent is $550 a month." "I can afford that, Steve." "I require two months' security in advance." "I think I can manage that." "I would also require that you sign a lease for one year, and every year after that we would negotiate another lease. When do you think you can move in, Pat?" "I think I can move by the end of the month." "I would need you to come to my house, and I will sign a rental agreement and give you a set of keys." "That sounds good to me, Steve." You work at Delacroix's, right, Pat?" Pat nodded in response. "So you can walk to work instead of having to drive back and forth from your parents' house. Where do they live?" "My parents' house is in Newcastle." "I live in Millbury on Southwest Avenue. It is the third road on the right side of University Avenue. The house number is 23. I would like you to come over tonight at eight." "I'll be there, Steve," Pat said as they shook hands. As Pat walked back to his car, he hoped that his parents would be happy that he had found a place to live on his own. It was a little impulsive, he thought, to agree to rent an apartment without checking first with his parents. They said that they would help him with the security deposit. He hoped that they would be supportive of his decision. When Pat came home that evening, he told his parents about the apartment. "I saw a house this morning on my way to Delacroix's, and I called the owner during my break. I said that I would rent it from him. It's relatively close to Delacroix's, so I can walk to work almost every day." "We said that we would help with the security deposit, Pat," his mother said. "How much is the monthly rent?" "We agreed that it would $550 a month." "Your father and I have set aside some money for this situation. What I recommend that you do is bring your checkbook with you, so that way your check will serve as a receipt. Tomorrow you can deposit the money that Dad will give you tonight to cover your security deposit. Do you want Dad to go with you, Pat?" "No, I'll be okay." "Where does the landlord live, Pat?" his father asked. "He lives in Millbury, on a side street off University Avenue." At seven that evening, Pat drove to Steve's house in Millbury. He was excited that he was finally to be able to live independently, and that his parents were supportive of his endeavor. He walked up the sidewalk and rang the doorbell. Steve opened the door and gave him a hearty handshake. "Welcome, Pat. Please come into my house." Steve escorted him to his office. There was a chair placed in front of Steve's enormous oak desk. "Have a seat. Would you like a cup of coffee to celebrate?" Pat was a little uneasy, and he decided a cup of coffee might help him calm down. "Yes, thanks, Steve," he replied. While Steve was making a cup of coffee for him, Pat remained sitting in the chair. Steve walked into his office, carrying a tray. Besides two empty cups on it, there was also a carafe, a sugar bowl, a creamer, and two spoons. Steve set the tray down on the table, poured into the coffee a cup, and handed it to him. "There's milk and sugar if you like." "It's fi ne the way it is, Steve. I like my coffee black." "I need a little milk and sugar in mine to make it appetizing," Steve said as he poured himself a cup and added a little of each to his. "Let's toast this special occasion, Pat." Steve said as he sat down facing him. Steve raised his cup and touched it against Pat's cup, making a clinking sound. "Now, let's get down to business. Here is a copy of the lease." Steve handed Pat a sheet of paper. "I'm going to read aloud from it, so follow along with me." After he finished reading from it, Steve had Pat sign in the appropriate places on both sheets. Then Steve signed the forms, also. "Do you have any questions?" "No, Steve, I don't have any." "Please make a check payable to me for $1,650." Pat took out his checkbook, wrote out a check for that amount, payable to Steve, and handed it to him. "Here are your keys. You have a key for the front door and a key for the inside door leading into your apartment. Congratulations!" Steve rose to his feet, and Pat followed suit. Pat put the keys into his pocket before shaking hands with Steve. Then Steve led him to the front door and Pat walked to his car. Pat moved out of his parents' house and into the new apartment in Millbury at the end of August of that year. He rented a U-Haul truck and began packing it with all his personal belongings such as clothes, books, movies, CDs, and other items. He put the cartons in the U-Haul before the furniture he was taking with him: the bed, bureau, bookcase, and desk. When he was finished that Saturday morning, Pat said, "I'm ready to move to my new apartment, Mom and Dad." "Good luck, Pat," his father said as he shook hands with him. His mother gave him a kiss on the cheek. "Give us a call when you are settled in, Pat," she said. "We will pick you up this afternoon so that you can drive your car to your new apartment." As his parents stood in the garage, they watched as Pat opened the door to the truck and got behind the steering wheel. He waved to them, and they waved back to him.

CHAPTER NINE

After Pat reached his new apartment in Millbury, he parked the truck in the driveway. He began unloading his furniture from it: his bed, his bureau, his bookcase, his desk, a couch for the living room, his TV set, and finally a kitchen table set. He arranged his bedroom furniture in a way that was convenient for him before placing the couch against a wall in the living room. He set the TV set against the opposite wall, facing the couch. Then he placed the kitchen table and its accompanying chairs in the center of his kitchen. Pat decided to take the cartons from the truck and place them on the floor of the living room. Then he took out the contents from them and placed them in the proper locations: the books in the bookcase, the dishes, silverware, glassware, and pots in the kitchen cupboards. After he set up his apartment the way he liked it, he dialed his parents' telephone number on his cell phone. His mother answered his call. When he recognized her voice, he said, "Hello, Mom. I finished moving in." "Okay, Pat. Your father and I will drive your car this afternoon. Then we will take care of the U-Haul truck for you. We cannot wait for you to show us your new apartment. See you soon," his mother responded. Twenty minutes later Pat heard a knock on the front door. His parents were waiting outside, eager to see how his apartment was decorated. "Come in, Mom and Dad." He held open the front door to the house and they stepped into the front vestibule. "My apartment is on the right." He opened the heavy wooden door and they entered the living room. "Let me take you on a tour." From the living room was the entrance to the kitchen, and a small storage area off the kitchen. Going back to the living room, he escorted them through a hallway that had a door to the bathroom. He opened the door so they could see it. Finally, at the end of the hallway was the bedroom. There was a closet that ran the half the length of one wall. "It looks rather comfortable for you, Pat," his father said. "We hope you will be happy here." "Your father and I will drive the U-Haul truck for you," his mother said. "We're happy that you are on your own." "Thanks for taking care of the U-Haul truck," Pat replied. He opened the door that led into the foyer of the house and they walked towards the front door. "When do you go to work at Delacroix's, Pat?" his mother asked while they were walking to his parents' car and the U-Haul truck. As Pat gave his father the key to the U-Haul truck, he said, "On Monday afternoon at one, Mom." "Goodbye, Pat," his parents said as they opened the doors of their car and the U-Haul truck. Pat waved to them as they backed out of the driveway. Then he went inside his apartment, sat on his couch, and watched TV. It was a way to relax after the tension of moving and unpacking. A half hour later, he heard a knock on the door. He opened it carefully, uncertain who was on the other side of it. It was Steve. Standing next to him was a man not yet thirty years old. "Pat, I thought I would introduce you to your upstairs neighbor. This is Mike Andrews. Mike, this is Pat Kavanaugh. He moved in today." "It's nice to meet you, Pat," Mike said as he extended his hand to Pat. "Nice to meet you also, Mike," Pat said as they shook hands. "I wanted the two of you to get acquainted with each other so that you can depend on one another for help," Steve said as he and Mike entered Pat's apartment. "There's also a third tenant on the top floor, above Mike's apartment, but she's not home. Mike can introduce you to her, Pat. I'll see you two later, guys," Steve said before leaving Pat's apartment, closing the door behind him. Mike sat down on Pat's couch. "Mike, would you like a drink?" Pat said as he opened the refrigerator. "What do you have, Pat?" "I have milk, soda, orange juice, and spring water." "I'll have a glass of soda. Do you have any ice for it?" "Yes. How many ice cubes do you want in your glass?' "Three, please." Pat poured the soda into two glasses before opening the freezer and pulling out the ice cube tray. Using a set of tongs, he dropped three ice cubes into Mike's glass. Then he put two ice cubes into his own glass before coming into the living room. He handed one glass to Mike before sitting down in his armchair. "Welcome to the neighborhood, Pat," Mike said. The next two hours flew by as they engaged in small talk about sports, their jobs, the news, and other topics. Then Mike said, "It was nice to meet you, Pat. I hope you enjoy living here." Rising to his feet, he said, "I have to get going." Pat stood up and they walked together to the door. Pat opened it and Mike stepped into the foyer of the house. "I'm glad to have you as a neighbor, Mike. Take care." Then he closed the door as Mike climbed the stairs to his apartment. On Monday afternoon, Pat walked to work. He really enjoyed having the chance to save money by not driving his car as much to go to work at the store. As usual, Mr. Harris was waiting for him by the time clock. "Mr. Harris, I moved to an apartment in Millbury. Would you like to have my new address for my personnel file?" Pat said as he punched in. "Yes, I would." Pat wrote down his address on a piece of paper and handed it to Mr. Harris, who said, "I see that you can walk to work. That's a good thing for me to know, Pat." "Why is that, Mr. Harris?" "Because I can call you to come to work in a moment's notice. You will not have the opportunity to tell me that you cannot. I will expect you to drop everything and come to work immediately. I also need you to work this coming Labor Day. I want to be with my family that day. We're invited to a cookout with my wife's brother and his family." "I've already worked three holidays this year, Mr. Harris." "Remember when you asked for that day off some time ago? Well, it is my turn to ask you to return the favor. It goes both ways." "All right, I guess. It's just ironic to have to work on the day created to honor the working people." "Now, Pat, don't have an attitude. Do you know how many people would like to be gainfully employed? As I see it, you are very lucky to have a job here. Do not do anything to risk losing it, such as how you speak to me. Understand?" Mr. Harris fixed an angry glare in Pat's direction. "Yes, Mr. Harris. I understand." "Good. I will schedule you for Friday,

Saturday, Sunday, and Monday. Let's get to work. Come with me to our department because I have projects for you to do this afternoon and tonight." As they walked to the celebrations department, Pat wondered to himself what he did wrong to deserve Mr. Harris as a supervisor. It must be some sort of cosmic retribution, he thought to himself. It was becoming necessary to escape from not only the clutches of this individual, but also from Delacroix's, because a bachelor's degree did not automatically warrant a higher salary. Yet he knew to be careful not to fall out of the frying pan and into the fire. It was not that he did not want to work, but he found the working conditions at Delacroix's increasingly becoming a burden to him. Pat decided to call Sean one night after work. He dialed his friend's number on his cell phone, eagerly waiting for him to answer his call. The ringing on the other end was interrupted by Sean's enthusiastic voice answering, "Hello?" Pat said, "Sean, it's Pat." "Hey, Pat! How are you?" "Sean, I'm fi ne. Thanks for asking. And you?" "Okay. So, what's new?" "I moved into my apartment in Millbury. It is the first floor of a house on a side street off University Avenue. I can walk to work every day and save money on gas." "That sounds great, Pat!" "Thanks, Sean. You can come over and visit sometime." They talked for a few more minutes before Sean said, "I must hang up now, Pat. It was nice talking to you." "I'll give you a call later on to invite you over, Sean. Goodbye," Pat said. "Goodbye, Pat," Sean said before hanging up the phone. Pat decided he needed to create a budget. Turning on his laptop, he opened Microsoft Excel and on the screen was a new worksheet. He entered estimated costs of necessities: rent, electricity, insurance for his car and apartment, newspaper, credit cards, food, clothing and telephone, which included his cell phone and access to the Internet. His monthly wage was $1,480, based on a forty-hour workweek at $9.25 an hour, before taxes, and other deductions. He figured that any remaining funds could be deposited into a savings account. He believed that at least he was on his way to achieving the American Dream. Pat adjusted to life on his own for the most part very well: walking to work and back, and managing his finances by having his paycheck electronically deposited at the Savings Bank of Millbury. He also found it more convenient to have his checking account electronically debited for expenses rather than writing paper checks. The only checks he wrote were to his property owner, any food purchases he made at Delacroix's, and to All Saints Church, where he joined as a parishioner and requested offertory envelopes.

CHAPTER TEN

Now that Pat was a parishioner at All Saints Church, he tried to get to know not only Father Pawlowski, but also the other members of the parish community. After the concluding rite of the Mass one Sunday morning, Father announced, "I welcome all of you to come to the Parish Hall for coffee and doughnuts." Pat followed the other parishioners to the Parish Hall, located through a side door near the entrance vestibule of All Saints Church. Tables and chairs were set up, and people were milling about, deciding where to sit. Pat took a napkin and a plate and then used the napkin to select a doughnut and put it on the plate. Then he chose a cup of freshly brewed coffee from several placed on a table next to the basket of doughnuts. Looking around the room, he spotted a table where a few other people about his age were sitting. Before pulling out a chair, he said, "I'd like to join you at this table. May I sit here?" "Be my guest," said a young man. "Hi. I'm John Blodgett and this is my wife Kelly." Pat put down his coffee and doughnut on the table and sat across from John and Kelly. "Pleased to meet you. I'm Pat Kavanaugh." "Have you always attended Masses at All Saints Church, Pat?" John asked. "When I was a student at NSU several years ago, my roommate and I went to Mass on a regular basis, and then when I moved to Millbury so I could continue working at Delacroix's, I came back to All Saints Church." Kelly said, "Now I know where I have seen you. When you came over to the table, I recognized you but I couldn't quite remember where." "Yes, you've probably seen me at Delacroix's, Kelly." Next to Kelly was a young woman who smiled at Pat. "I've seen you at Delacroix's also, Pat," she said. "I'm Stacey Norris. Welcome to All Saints Church." Father Pawlowski approached them while they were talking. "Hello, Father," John said. "Have you met Pat Kavanaugh?" Pat stood up as Father extended his hand to him. "It's nice to see young people like you attending Mass on a weekly basis." "My parents taught me the responsibility of attending Mass every week," Pat replied. "When I was an on-campus resident at NSU, I went to Mass with my roommate every Sunday. I remember Father O'Connell." "I became pastor when he was transferred to another parish. If there is anything the Parish staff or I can do for you, please let me know." "Thanks, Father. I will keep that in mind." "Kelly and I have to get going now, Pat," John said as they stood up. "It was great meeting you." "I enjoyed getting to know you and your wife, John," Pat said. After they left, Pat and Stacey continued talking to become better acquainted with one another. He said, "I graduated from NSU here in Millbury last year, Stacey." "What a coincidence. I'm also a graduate of NSU. My major was social work. I am now pursuing a master's degree. I live with my family in Millbury, so I commute to NSU. With so many people attending NSU, I suppose that we never had a chance to meet one another until now." After talking to one another for a few minutes while enjoying their coffee and doughnuts, Stacey said, "You seem like a nice guy to hang out with, Pat." She opened her purse and took out a pad of paper. Ripping off a sheet, she wrote down her telephone number. "Give me a call sometime. We can go out for dinner." Then she stood up and pushed in her chair. "I must go home. Pat, I look forward to hearing from you." "I plan to do that, Stacey," Pat said as he stood up and pushed in his chair. He followed her to the parking lot behind the church. As they got into their cars, they waved at one another. As Pat drove home, it occurred to him that Stacey could be a good choice for him romantically. He thought, they belonged to the same church, and they were about the same age. I hope this works out well for me, he thought as he continued the drive home. His parents would be proud of him for finding a young woman to love and marry. On Thursday night of that week, Pat made a phone call to Stacey. "How would you like to go out for dinner tomorrow night?" "Yes, Pat, I would like that very much. How about the University Avenue Grill at 6:30? It's a new restaurant that opened recently." "I can meet you there, Stacey," Pat replied. "Great. I'll see you then." She hung up the telephone. While Pat was working the next morning at Delacroix's, he thought that he was lucky to meet Stacey. He wasn't planning to have a girlfriend at that point, but he was open to having one. He was looking forward to having dinner with her and a chance to get to know her better. After coming home on Friday afternoon, Pat changed from his work uniform and wore a dark blue shirt with matching slacks and shoes. He was excited at the thought that Stacey just might be the one for him. Driving to the restaurant, he imagined a life with her: a house, children and a dog or a cat. Stacey was waiting for him when he entered the restaurant. "I arrived a few minutes ago, Pat," she said as she extended her hand to him. A young woman greeted them. "Two guests?" She led them to a table by a window. "Joey will be your server, folks," she said as she handed them their menus. Joey arrived soon after at their table. "Can I get you anything to drink while you're looking over the menus?" Stacey replied, "I'd like a diet soda, please." "I'll have a coffee, please," Pat said. "So many good choices, Pat. I don't know which one to get," Stacey said after she sipped her soda. "I think I'll have the hamburger with the works," Pat said. "That sounds good." Joey came back with their drinks. Placing them on the table, he asked, "Ready to order, miss?" Stacey said, "I'll have the BLT." Pat said, "I'll have the hamburger with the works." "Coming right up, folks," Joey said as he finished taking their orders. After he left, Stacey said, "How long have you been working at Delacroix's?" Pat replied, "About five years now. I started while I was attending NSU, on the advice of my advisor. She suggested that I work there to get some experience." They continued talking to one another on a variety of subjects while waiting for Joey to come to their table with their dinners. After he served them, they continued their discussion as a means of getting to know one another. After they were finished eating, Joey approached them and asked, "Anything else?" Pat and

Stacey looked at one another before shaking their heads. Pat said, "I think we're ready for the check, please." "Okay." Joey put the check on the table. Pat looked at it and took out his wallet. As he removed a credit card from it, Stacey said, "Let me reimburse you for my portion of it." "I thought it was customary for the man to pay for the meal when dining out with a woman." "I can't let you pay for me, because you work at Delacroix's and you can't afford to buy me dinner. If you want to make me happy, please don't think of this meal as a date. I only want a friendship with you." Stacey removed several bills from her purse and handed them to him. "This should cover my meal plus the tip, Pat." "How did you arrive at the conclusion that I couldn't afford to pay for you, Stacey?" Pat asked as he took the bills from her and put them in his wallet. Then he placed his credit card on the table with the check. Stacey hesitated for a minute before giving him an answer. Not wanting to admit that she wanted them to remain just friends, she said, "We'll talk about that later." Joey came over to their table and took both items for processing. When he came back, he had Pat sign the slip. "Thank you for dining out at the University Avenue Grill, folks. Come back again." Pat and Stacey stood up and walked out of the restaurant. "Thanks for understanding my viewpoint regarding tonight's dinner. I'm just not ready for a dating relationship." "Well, I had a good time with you nonetheless, Stacey." As he was about to embrace her, she moved out of his reach and placed a quick peck on his cheek. Then they went to their cars. They drove out of the parking lot while waving at each other. That night Pat called Sean. "I met a young woman at All Saints Church recently, and she is a graduate student at NSU. She is in the process of obtaining a master's degree in social work." "Did you go out with her, Pat?" "We went to the University Avenue Grill for dinner tonight. For some reason she insisted on reimbursing me for her part of the check. She said that she wasn't ready to go on a date with me. I think she is hiding something from me." "Perhaps she has a boyfriend, and she didn't want to admit that to you." "That's a possibility. However, she claimed that I couldn't afford to take her out because I work at Delacroix's." "I don't know what to tell you, Pat," Sean said. "It's getting late, and I have to go to bed soon. Talk to you later." "Take care, Sean," Pat said as he hung up the phone. Pat continued going out with Stacey to various recreational activities: movies, miniature golf, visiting museums, and driving to see picturesque sites such as Gillette Castle and Heublein Tower. She always insisted that she pay her own way; she wouldn't let him pay for her. Moreover, she was adamant on doing all the driving; she would pick up and drop off Pat at his apartment whenever they went out. He got the impression that she delineated the limits of their friendship; under no circumstances was it ever going to evolve into a courtship, for reasons unknown to him.

CHAPTER ELEVEN

After two years of working full-time at Delacroix's, Pat was getting very frustrated that despite the work ethic that he learned from his father, he wasn't getting paid more based on the number of years of employment. Seniority did not play a role as much as work performance did in terms of financial compensation. He felt he was doing his best, but it just did not work in his favor. Although Mr. Delacroix had previously explained to him his policy regarding wages and salaries when Pat went from part-time to full-time, he felt he was not being paid enough to make ends meet. Moreover, his salary was not keeping up with unforeseen expenses, and he found himself relying on his credit cards to pay for these bills. He remembered Mr. Delacroix's caution considering the elimination of luxuries. These extenuating circumstances forced him to live paycheck to paycheck. He was under the impression he had only himself to blame that he wasn't living within his means, when in reality it was beyond his control. His income was slipping through his fingers. As time went by, he discovered that his university education was becoming obsolete, because he was unable to apply the knowledge he'd learned at Delacroix's, despite knowing that he had the capability. Unfortunately, due to Mr. Delacroix's rigid policy, he was unable to demonstrate his competence. He thought about obtaining an MBA, but that would only make him overqualified to work at

Delacroix's and it might be perceived as a threat to take Mr. Harris' position as the celebrations manager. The experience that he'd hoped to gain to support his bachelor's degree could not be obtained, due to the tough labor market. However, he could not cut back much on anything because there were few remaining personal indulgences. He was made to feel that living beyond his budget was entirely his own fault; he had nobody to blame but himself for his financial predicament. The crushing load of debt, which had a snowballing effect as far as he was concerned, was a considerable factor in his desire to find a higher-paying position, because he knew that his chances of advancement at Delacroix's were nonexistent. To make matters worse, it seemed to him that he was financially lagging his fellow college graduates, although he never kept in touch with any of them except Sean. While there was no realistic basis for this opinion, he felt that he wasn't measuring up to the standards dictated by society in general. The idea in his mind was that he was always behind the eight ball: every attempt to pay down a credit card balance only triggered a higher balance on another credit card. It was a vicious circle with no end in sight. Stacey also added fuel to the fire that was burning inside him. Although she made it clear that their friendship was purely platonic, she felt that she had the right to push him to demand more money from Mr. Delacroix. One day, while they were driving on Route 2 to go to Mystic, she said, "I hope that Mr. Delacroix is paying you at least eleven dollars an hour, because you've been working there at least eight years now." "Why would you ask such a question, Stacey? You've decided that because I work at Delacroix's that, in your opinion, I can't afford to spend money on you, but then you feel it's your business to inquire about my salary. You can't have it both ways." "I was only trying to help you. I felt bad that Mr. Delacroix was trying to take advantage of you." "Unfortunately, because of the tough labor market, I don't really have a choice. I really don't want to talk about it, Stacey. Let's just forget about it." "Okay. I won't discuss it anymore, Pat," Stacey said while driving on the highway. At a quarter per hour raise each year, grudgingly doled out, Pat still hadn't hit the maximum wage of ten dollars an hour, which was the limit for his grade, according to Mr. Delacroix's pay scale. No matter how hard he tried to apply himself and demonstrate that he was more capable of positions in the store that were higher paying, it never merited the attention of Mr. Delacroix. He came to the reluctant conclusion that Mr. Delacroix was true to his word about advancing his associates up the store's corporate ladder. Pat was hoping that Mr. Delacroix could make an exception for him, so that his father would be pleased that a university education would finally pay off. However, it was not meant to be, he finally realized. It was either Mr. Delacroix's way or the highway, and he was not sure which way to turn. During this time, Pat stayed in touch with Sean, who assured him that life would be better eventually. He enjoyed talking to his former university roommate on a regular basis. Every so often, they got together for lunch on weekends. Exhausted from applying for positions through newspapers and other sources, only to receive rejections letters and postcards, Pat decided on a different strategy: a professional employment coach. Searching online through different websites, he found one in the downtown section of Mapleton. He sent his résumé via his e-mail server, and Mr. Morgan, the owner of a career development business, sent him a response inviting him to his office. On the day of his appointment, Pat was very excited at the prospect of this perhaps life-changing event. If all went well, he thought to himself, he would be able to leave Delacroix's and go onto something that would compensate him in terms of a higher wage. Having a university degree should count for something, he thought as he put on a three-piece suit and tie. As Pat drove to his appointment in Mapleton, he visualized a better life opening up for him: a well-paying job that did not require him to be available at all hours of the day, but rather an eight-to-five work schedule, with no weekends, nights, and holidays, a loving wife and children, and his own home rather than an apartment. Reaching the building where Mr. Morgan's office was located, he parked his car in the adjacent parking lot and walked to the front of the building. He was looking for Morgan Career & Résumé Services. A sign in the lobby indicated that it was in Suite 229. He took an elevator to the second floor of the building, the doors opened, and he stepped into the hallway. He turned left and walked down the corridor until he came to the correct suite. He opened the door and found himself in a waiting room, much like at a doctor's office. Rows of folding chairs lined the four walls of the waiting room. Decorating the walls were various motivational posters, illustrated with scenes of nature. The captions below the photos were phrases intended to inspire morale. Chairs surrounded a coffee table brimming with career magazines and newspapers. Another door opened off the waiting room. Nobody else was in the room, so he took a seat and waited for Mr. Morgan to open the door to his private office and greet him. After five minutes of waiting, which seemed like a long time to Pat, the inner door opened and a man came into the waiting room. He was professionally dressed and had brown hair parted to the left side. There was a hint of gray at the temples. A pair of reading glasses was perched on his nose. "Are you Pat Kavanaugh?" "Yes, sir." "Nice to meet you. I am Skip Morgan. Come into my office." He escorted Pat into his office. At first, Pat stood after entering it. He waited until Skip took a seat behind the enormous desk. "Please, have a seat, Pat. Do not be so nervous. It's going to be all right." Pat privately wondered what kind of a name Skip was. He guessed it was a nickname of some sort, and he realized that the man preferred to be called Skip. He resisted the inclination to ask the man what his birth name was, because there would be the temptation to address him by that name rather than the preferred nickname. "I was looking over your résumé prior to your appointment with me this morning, and unfortunately I really can't place you in a position that pays more than what you are getting at Delacroix's, Pat." "So what did I do wrong, Skip?" A worried look came over Pat's face. He was afraid that his education was wasted. "I wouldn't come to the conclusion that you didn't do anything right or wrong; it has to do with the timing. The dilemma that you are facing is the result of a very tight labor market, with a large number of candidates competing for the same spot. It was beyond your control, and this predicament that you are facing isn't your fault." "But my parents feel that this situation is something that I brought on myself." "They shouldn't blame you; it's just an unfortunate course of events. There was nothing you could do to avert it." "So what do you recommend, Skip?" "Well, you can work part-time." "There's just one problem, Skip." "What's that?" "I'm not allowed to have a part-time job. Mr. Delacroix expects me to be available every day from eight A.M. until eleven P.M. He does not allow his associates to have set schedules. It would be impossible for me to coordinate a parttime job to avoid schedule conflicts." "I understand that he seems inflexible in his scheduling of your shifts. However, there is a method to work around that. I really want to help you. I know someone who is actively searching for people who want to be their own bosses. He can help you set up your own business. You will be provided with the right tools and he will support you, but you have to take the initiative. When you earn more money by being successfully self-employed, you will be able to break free from the domination that you are experiencing currently. You won't need to be dependent on Mr. Delacroix for employment." "But what about benefits such as health insurance? I was under the impression that to have health insurance, I needed to have an employer to take care of it for me. I would have to buy it myself?" "Look at this way. Yes, you would have to pay for it yourself, but it would be better than working for peanuts at Delacroix's. You have fallen into the trap of letting your employer take care of you. Let me make a guess: you have learned this method from your parents. You believe that by having a university education will pave the way for the good things in life, such as having a secure job, employer-sponsored benefits and not having to worry about gaps in unemployment. The times have changed, Pat." "Are you suggesting that I be my own boss, Skip?" "While you would be working for yourself, you wouldn't be working by yourself. If it's okay with you, I would like to have Dan Kelly, an acquaintance of mine, give you a phone call and he can discuss with the business opportunity that he has," Skip replied. Pat squirmed in his chair, unsure about what Skip was saying. After a minute of deliberating, he said, "Yes, Skip. Have Dan Kelly call me." "I'm glad that you are being proactive with the opportunity. Trust me; this will be life-changing, Pat." Skip stood up and shook hands with Pat. "Everything will work out all right, Pat. It can't get any worse than right now. Good luck." Pat replied, "Thanks, Skip." Then he stepped into the corridor and walked out of the building to his car in the parking lot. As he drove home, he wondered about Dan Kelly and his business opportunity. He was a little disappointed that his meeting with Skip Morgan did not pan out as he hoped. It was discouraging to be told that his university education did not guarantee a higher-paying job. About an hour after he came home, his cell phone rang. "Hello?" he answered. "I'm looking for Pat Kavanaugh, please," a man's voice replied. "This is Pat. May I help you?" "Hello, Pat. This is Dan Kelly. I received your name from a contact, Skip Morgan. How are you doing?" "I'm fi ne, Mr. Kelly. And you?" "I'm doing well. Thanks for asking." "I'm glad that you called. Skip said that you would get in touch with me. Could you tell me a little about the opportunity regarding your business, Dan?" Pat said. "I prefer not to get involved with the specifics over the telephone. Suffice it to say I am inviting you to an informational session tomorrow night at 7:00 at my office, located in Mapleton, on Hillside Avenue. It is in an office building, number 80, Suite 225. Do you think you can be available then? I hope so." "Yes, Dan. I am free tomorrow night, so I would like to come to it. Thanks for inviting me," Pat replied. "You should come dressed professionally. See you then, Pat." "I'll be there. Goodbye, Dan." "Goodbye, Pat." The following day, while Pat worked at Delacroix's, he thought about the opportunity being presented to him. It seemed like a good idea at the time. At least, it seemed to being an improvement compared to working at Delacroix's, where he never got a chance to be promoted up the career ladder. So on the following night, Pat was dressed in the business suit he wore on the day he first met Skip. He drove to 80 Hillside Avenue in Mapleton. Parking in the lot next to the building, he locked his car before entering the building. Suite 225 was located on the second floor. Climbing the stairs to the second floor, he opened the door and walked into a narrow corridor. Mounted on the wall facing him were signs indicating which direction to turn to find suite 225. He chose the left turn and walked down the hallway until he came to the suite on the right side of the corridor. As he came into the vicinity of the suite, he could hear quiet voices and restrained chuckling. He wondered to himself if this was a good opportunity for him. Pat quietly opened the door and found people of all ages and races milling about in a room that had rows of folding chairs. He stood at the perimeter of the group, unsure how to blend in. He felt uneasy watching the others in the room conduct themselves with complete abandon. He focused on the walls, which, like the waiting room at Skip's office, were decorated with scenes of nature complemented by motivational phrases. As Pat entered the room, a middle-aged man wearing a business suit approached him. He had curly red hair and freckles. A pair of half-moons was attached to a chain around his neck. Green eyes focused on him. "You must be Pat. Welcome to my business of making peoples' dreams become a reality," Dan Kelly said as he offered his hand to Pat. "I'm glad you were able to come tonight. Relax, my friend," Dan put his hands on Pat's shoulders. "Allow me to introduce you to my associates." Grabbing him by his arm, Dan led him around, having him meet the others assembled in the room. After each person was presented to Pat, there was the obligatory handshake along with the expression, "Pleased to meet you, Pat." None of the individuals who encountered Pat strayed from this custom. Pat said in return, upon meeting each of Dan's associates, "I'm glad to meet you also." He was very careful to address the individuals properly. Dan made his way to the podium in the front of the room. Speaking into the microphone attached to it, he said, "All right, let's get down to business. Everybody, please take a seat." Everyone in the room sat down in the chairs. Dan's booming voice echoed through the room as he said, "Everybody, please welcome Pat Kavanaugh to our group. Pat, please stand up." Pat rose to his feet as everybody, including Dan, clapped. "This is Pat's first time at our meeting. We hope he will be successful enough to tell his boss to take a flying leap!" "Hear, hear!" A man shouted those words in Pat's direction. "Okay, Pat. You can take a seat now. It's awards time!" Dan continued speaking at the podium. He picked up a trophy and announced, "This goes to a young woman who has been with us for about two months, and she has been successful in her appointments. In only her second month, she earned over a thousand dollars in sales. Let's hear it for Julianne Trowbridge!" As Julianne walked to the podium, Dan shook her hand and handed to her the trophy. It was personally inscribed. As she stood at the podium, she said, "Thank you, everybody in this room, for all your support and encouragement. I couldn't have achieved this award without your support!" The room was filled emphatic applause. Pat thought it would be stupendous if he were one day at the podium receiving accolades. After Julianne left the podium with her trophy and returned to her seat, Dan called on other people to come, receive a trophy, and give a speech. Everyone also was applauded for his or her performance. After the meeting was over and the others left the room with their trophies, Dan asked Pat, "What do you think?" "I have never seen so much enthusiasm in my entire life. All these people can accomplish quite a lot." "In a few months, you could be up in front of the room, accepting a personalized trophy for your performance — something that Mr. Delacroix could never do for you. How many times has he thanked you for a job well done, Pat?" Pat realized that in all his years of working at Delacroix's, he had never been thanked at all. Making a circle with his thumb and middle finger, he said, "None." "That's my point, Pat. I'm going to get you set up to work as one of my associates." Dan escorted Pat past the podium to a door on the far side of the room. Opening the door, he led Pat into another room. "Have a seat in front of my desk." Pat sat down in the straight-back chair as Dan sat in the black swivel chair behind his desk. "Skip Morgan told me that you work full-time at Delacroix's and that your schedule has no measure of predictability. I can help you earn a little income on the side in a way that does not interfere with his inflexible scheduling of your shifts. Each week, you will report your shift schedule to me, and I will find a way to accommodate you. At first, it will not seem to be that much, but as you get the ball rolling you will be able to leave Delacroix's with your held high. You will not be able to quit right away, but you will able to develop confidence in yourself gradually. Don't worry about it." "What kind of business did you have in mind for me, Dan?" "I'm glad you asked. I think you would do well as a sales facilitator in computer security." "What does that mean?" "To make a long story short, you would go into the fi eld with me, as your trainer, to prospective clients to complete at least one of two opportunities: (1) sell software dedicated to protect the computers of private clients from being compromised via the Internet or (2) sell computer maintenance contracts to customers who have out-of-warranty computers. My organization, DK and

Associates, is associated with a corporation called CompSec Nationwide, which provides these services to private consumers. I do not actually work for CompSec Nationwide, but I facilitate their services to the individuals through my organization. " "And how would I find these individuals, Dan?" "They're right in your backyard: neighbors, friends, and acquaintances. You and I would go to their houses and show them the products that would help them protect their computers. I work with other people who, like you, found themselves needing to earn a little extra money on a part-time basis. Eventually they were able to quit their day jobs and work for themselves under my guidance. I would like you to consider my proposal. It could change your life, Pat." "I think I would like to do that, Dan." "Well, I think you made the right decision. In addition, the best part is, it only costs $299 to get involved, and it is fully refundable upon completion of six successful training sessions. You will see that it pays for itself." "What's the point of requiring me to pay for this opportunity, when I will get back my start-up fee?" Pat asked. He was a little concerned as to what might happen if he were to fork over any amount of money to unreliable individuals. His father had warned him to watch out for con artists looking to make a quick buck. However, there seemed to be a legitimate product behind the opportunity, so keeping that in his mind eased his concerns. "The model used by us as facilitators of CompSec Nationwide is based on the belief that a business requires a sense of capital investment. It makes the opportunity all the more meaningful to you, the newly self-employed business owner. You have already met some of my associates and you saw for yourself their successes in action. If they can follow through and be persistent in their efforts, so can you. The only person who would be holding you back is…" he took a deep breath before continuing, "… is you." "I guess you're on target about me," Pat replied. Opening a filing cabinet next to his desk, Dan pulled out a manila folder. Taking out one of the blank forms printed with the letterhead CompSec Nationwide, he presented it to Pat, and directed that Pat fill it out. It was a contract between Dan's company and Pat. One of the conditions specified was the successful completion of six no-purchase-required training sessions with acquaintances. "I don't know if I can do that.

That's something my father warned me about." "That's negative thinking. Remember; think positive and you will be positive. All those people you saw earlier this evening were all full of enthusiasm. Most importantly, they overcame obstacles to succeed. You can too, if you just put your mind to it." Dan saw the uncertainty in Pat's face fade away to self-confidence. "That's the spirit." Pat began filling the form out as Dan started to gather materials: books such as Dale Carnegie's bestselling book How to Win Friends and Influence People, pamphlets, a CD, and a DVD for Pat's reference. When Pat was finished entering the information on the form, he signed it. Dan also signed it before making a copy of it on his fax machine. "Now I need $299 as a start-up fee. I can take credit cards, Pat." Pat opened his wallet and took out a credit card. He handed it to Dan, who used it to complete Pat's membership in the business. After handing the credit card back to Pat, he said, "Welcome to the business, Pat." Dan stood up. Pat also stood up. "I'm glad that I am making an effort to be my own boss and not let someone like Mr. Harris push me around for his own egotistical needs. I am going to leave now, Dan." "Just keep me informed about your schedule so that I can help you achieve your goal of breaking free from Delacroix's, Pat. Please give me the names of anybody that you might know, so I can set up a meeting with them. I am not your supervisor, but your coach. I will work for you, so that you can succeed." Dan gave him a business card. "Here is my contact information: cell phone number, fax number, and my e-mail address." "Thanks, Dan." Pat put Dan's business card in his pocket before leaving the office. He walked to his car, carrying the materials that Dan provided him. Then he went home, hoping that his life would get better fi nancially. The next night after work, Pat decided to call Sean to tell him about this enterprise. "Sean, I am going into business for myself." "Doing what, Pat?" Sean asked. "It's a business opportunity. I would be offering software dedicated to protect the computers of private clients from being compromised via the Internet, or offering computer maintenance contracts to customers who have out-of-warranty computers." "What do you mean by 'business opportunity'? Won't that conflict with Mr. Delacroix's policy about not working parttime?" "Mr. Delacroix doesn't have to know. I am not being paid on an hourly basis; instead, it is based on the business volume. The individual that I am working with, Dan Kelly, will help me get around my inflexible scheduling. Eventually, with the right training, I can be free of the deplorable working conditions at Delacroix's. All I had to do was to plunk down $299 as an investment in my future. And when I complete six sessions with Dan as my trainer, I will be reimbursed for the full amount." "Didn't your father warn you about those kinds of business opportunities, Pat?" "Sean, this is one is different. I'm offering products and services to people who have computers. There is a need for them." "Well, good luck, Pat. We'll talk later. Goodbye," Sean hung up his phone. I hope he doesn't solicit me for such a session, he thought to himself. Pat knew the names of his neighbors, so he used the telephone directory to look up their phone numbers. He felt that he could count on them, at the very least, to help him by allowing him and Dan to agree to have them over for a complimentary meeting. He also included Mike Andrews, his upstairs neighbor, on his list. Using Microsoft Word, he designed a table that listed their names and phone numbers. Then he e-mailed the document as an attachment to Dan. The accompanying message from Pat reported that he knew these people as neighbors. When Dan received the table from Pat, he first checked the mandatory do-not-call register to make sure none of the people on Pat's list was on it, to avoid punitive action. John Blodgett was the first name that he called. "Hello?" "Hello, is this Mr. Blodgett?" Dan asked. "Yes, that's me." "Mr. Blodgett, this is Dan Kelly. How are you?" "Fine, Dan. And you?" "I'm doing well Thanks for asking. I represent a company called Kelly and Associates. Do you know Pat Kavanaugh? He knows you from All Saints Church." John Blodgett said, "Yes, I know who he is. What can I do for you, sir?" "Pat recently went to work for himself as an independent business owner offering software dedicated to protect the computers of private clients from being compromised via the Internet, or offering computer maintenance contracts to customers who have out-of-warranty computers." Dan continued. "Would you be willing to have him and me over to your house for a complimentary demonstration? It would only take ten minutes of your time." "No, thank you. Whatever you are trying to sell, we are not buying it. We are not interested. Please do not call me again, Dan." John angrily hung up the phone. He was angry that Pat supplied his name to Dan. I thought he was a friend of mine, he thought to himself. Dan shook his head as he drew a line through John Blodgett's name on Pat's list. Not deterred by such lack of interest, he tried the second, third and fourth contacts. Each individual that Dan called expressed the same sentiment also. The last person he called on Pat's behalf was Mike, Pat's upstairs neighbor. Unfortunately, Mike was not very cooperative with Dan's request. After hanging up the phone with Dan, Mike rushed downstairs and angrily knocked on Pat's door. Pat opened the door and saw a red-faced Mike standing in front of it. "Did you have some guy call me to ask if I would be interested in maintenance contracts for my computer?" "Yes, Mike, I did. Was that a problem for you?" "It most certainly was! If I want that kind of service, I will get it myself. I do not need anybody to get it for me. Moreover, I do not appreciate you giving my name out to anyone else. Don't ever do that to me again!" Mike hollered as he walked away from Pat's door. Pat merely shut the door as Mike stormed to his apartment upstairs, bewildered by his outburst. He thought to himself, I am only following the model provided to me. I never expected this reaction from anybody. One day when Pat and Stacey were driving to see the covered bridge in West Cornwall, he said, "I recently became a facilitator for CompSec Nationwide." "What does that mean, Pat?" "It means that I work for myself, by arranging with a company to provide software dedicated to protect the computers of private clients from being compromised via the Internet, or offering computer maintenance contracts to customers who have out-of-warranty computers. I function as a liaison between the company and the client. I provide a list of my friends and neighbors to the man who recruited me, and he contacts them on my behalf." "Why did you get involved with him?" "I saw the opportunity to earn extra cash." "It seems to me that it's an opportunity all right ... to take advantage of your friends and neighbors." "What are you talking about, Stacey?" Pat turned to look at her. "I wouldn't like it if someone contacted me out of the blue in the manner that you're describing." "I have come across the resistance that you are referring to. I am trapped because I can't get a better-paying position at Delacroix's, because Mr. Delacroix has a policy about his pay scale. Also due to the economy no one is hiring for my skills, despite my bachelor's degree." "I don't like the sound of this method. Why are you trying to rip off your friends?" "First of all, I'm not ripping off my friends. I'm just trying to penetrate the warm market. Instead of making cold calls and knocking on doors, I have my recruiter contact my friends on my behalf." Stacey decided to change the subject. "I think you should know that I have completed my master's degree in social work." "What's the next step, Stacey?" "I have been applying for positions across the country. I had an interview with a not-for-profit clinic in New Jersey. They hired me. I am moving in a few weeks." Pat was stunned. All he could manage to say was, "Good luck." He was disappointed that since she was moving, their relationship could never advance to the boyfriend-girlfriend level. Although she had made it explicitly clear that they would always be friends and nothing more, he had hoped that she would change her mind. It was a parallel situation to the slimto-no chance of advancement up the ladder at Delacroix's. Stacey saw the worried look in his face. "Don't worry, Pat. We'll stay in touch. I must do what's best for me. You can always visit me and I could visit with you. We can send and receive e-mail messages every so often."

CHAPTER TWELVE

Stacey moved to Trenton, New Jersey and began working at the clinic that hired her two weeks after the journey to West Cornwall. While she would always remember the good times she had with Pat in their various excursions around Connecticut, she had to focus on her career and life in the Garden State. They tried to stay in touch, but the distance between them was insurmountable. To take his mind off losing Stacey as a potential girlfriend, he decided to keep building his business as a facilitator of CompSec Nationwide. He was constantly providing Dan with the contact information for individuals he was acquainted with, such as fellow parishioners at All Saints Church. However, he was very careful to omit the names of his fellow associates at Delacroix's. He did not want to risk the wrath of Mr. Delacroix, if the storeowner found out what he was doing. Mr. Delacroix might consider his actions as subversion. He attended the weekly meetings at Dan's office, hoping to continue having his enthusiasm for the opportunity in high gear, because it was important for him to get a refund at least on his start-up fee, as it was agreed in his contract with Dan. While his parents would not approve of such tactics, because they did not give out the names of their friends and relatives to anyone else, he needed to follow through. The opportunity was the only way out from the harsh circumstances that he experienced when working at Delacroix's. His father would also disapprove of his actions because he was trying to give something away for free, with no strings attached. In addition to the weekly meetings, Dan persuaded Pat to purchase motivational compact discs featuring lecturers who would expound on the art of making contacts for social and professional achievement. "You need to listen to these CDs to make your business grow. You can buy one from me each week. They will help you change your mindset, Pat," Dan said at the end of one such meeting. "Okay, Dan. I can't afford to miss out on such an opportunity," Pat replied. "I am investing in myself." One night Dan called Pat to tell him that he was arranging a seminar in a hotel located in the Berkshires in western Massachusetts. "It is important that you attend this conference, Pat." "When is it, Dan?" Pat looked at the calendar hanging in his kitchen. "It's three weeks from this coming Friday. It begins in the afternoon, and continues all day on Saturday and we leave on Sunday morning. You cannot afford to miss it, Pat. You'll have a good time up there." "I don't know if I can get that weekend off, Dan. I must ask my immediate manager for those days off. He is going to want to know why. I don't want to tell him the truth." "Just tell him it's personal, Pat." "Okay, Dan. I'll try that." "See you at the meeting this Thursday night?" "Yes, Dan. I'll be there." "Goodbye," Pat said as he hung up the phone. That night Pat decided he would put a request for those days off in a memo to Mr. Harris. He had learned how to design one in a clerical course he had taken at NSU. He put double spaces between the "to," "from," "re," and "date" lines. After moving the cursor down two lines, he entered the text expressing his request. When he was satisfi ed with the way he wrote his memo, he printed a copy. Then he created and printed a label and placed it on an envelope. After he folded the memo into thirds into the envelope, as he had learned in the clerical course, he sealed the flap. When Pat came into the store, Mr. Harris was stationed, as usual, by the time clock, waiting for him. "We have a lot of work to do this morning, Pat." "Good morning, Mr. Harris," Pat responded as he gave the envelope to his supervisor. "What's this?" Mr. Harris asked as he opened the envelope and pulled out the sheet of paper. "It's a request for time off. I am making it three weeks in advance, so you should be able to accommodate my request." "What if I don't want to? Are you going to be upset? You must be available at my discretion. I should not have to make a schedule change to accommodate your request. I schedule your shifts for my convenience, not yours. Remember, this job is your only priority." "It would be nice if you could be a little bit flexible instead of behaving as if you own me." "That's your first mistake. I do own you. Moreover, you can't go running to Mr. Delacroix, because he put me in charge of you." "Can't you at least offer me the courtesy of giving me a break? I really need to have these days off, Mr. Harris. Besides, isn't it customary for an associate to put in a request for a change in schedule at least two weeks in advance? It's not as if I waited until the schedule was posted and then came to you with this request." "In the first place, I schedule you for your weeks of vacation at my convenience. You are supposed to plan your necessary appointments accordingly. Moreover, couldn't this request for time off be arranged for when you would be on vacation, Pat? The policy that you are referring to does not pertain to you or any other associate at this store." Pat simply stared at Mr. Harris. He was in total disbelief in what he just heard. "You can't make an exception?" Finally, Mr. Harris relented. "All right, Pat. I will cave in this one time and pull some strings so that you will be off that weekend. I will put your memo on my desk. Now let's get going." Mr. Harris folded Pat's memo into the envelope and then stuffed it into his pocket. "But remember, you owe me a favor when I ask you. It goes both ways. I do something for you, and you must reciprocate when it is my turn. At some point you will have to do something for me, because I am your boss." He spoke as they walked to the celebrations department. Pat thought to himself as he walked behind Mr. Harris, As long as I continue working here, he's going to lord it over my head that he's my boss. I hope that this business opportunity will help me attain fi nancial independence. After work that afternoon, Pat called Dan about his success in arranging to have that weekend off. "Hello, Dan. It's Pat. I was able to work out an agreement with my manager so that I could be off for the weekend next month." "That's great news, Pat," Dan replied. "I'm going to give you directions to the hotel. It's in a town called Hancock, Massachusetts, near the New York state line. From northwestern Connecticut, you take US route 44 west to US route 7 north. Follow US route 7 over the Massachusetts state line into the town of Sheffield and continue north until you come to an intersection with Massachusetts state route 43, and you follow that. The Berkshire Motor Lodge is on the same road as the Hancock Shaker Village." "What time does this conference begin?" "The actual conference starts at 8. But you want to arrive as early as possible at the hotel. Be sure to book your room using the code 'DK and Associates.' The number for the hotel reservation desk is (413) 555-3476. I am looking forward to seeing you there. You'll make it to the top! Have a good night, Pat!" Dan enthusiastically hung up the phone. Pat found himself listening to a dial tone. Nonplussed by Dan's cryptic exhortation, Pat nevertheless dialed the number that was provided to him. A cheerful voice answered, "The Berkshire Motor Lodge. May I help you?" "Hello, this is Pat Kavanaugh. I would like to book a room for two nights next month. I was told to mention a code: DK and Associates." The desk clerk replied, "Thank you for providing me with that code. I can book for you a single occupancy room for Friday, May 4, and Saturday May 5. The cost is $129 for both nights and includes two complimentary breakfast buffets on Saturday and Sunday mornings. I will be glad to process your reservation using your credit card. Please be advised that a temporary hold will be placed on your credit card but it will not actually be charged until you check in on Friday afternoon. May I have your credit card number, please, Mr. Kavanaugh?" Pat took out his wallet and selected a credit card. "It will be a MasterCard, and the number is …." "Expiration date?" "May, 2012." "And for security purposes, the three numbers on the back of the credit card." Pat turned over the credit card and gave the desk clerk the three digits located on the signature panel. "Okay, Mr. Kavanaugh. You are all set. I will give you a confirmation number. Also, may I have an e-mail address so I can send you the information regarding your reservation?" "It's PKavanaugh1@galaxy.net." He spelled out each letter and number for the desk clerk. "Thanks, Mr. Kavanaugh." "You're welcome, sir," Pat said. He hung up the telephone on his desk before turning on his laptop. He checked his e-mail folder for the confirmation message from the

Berkshire Motor Lodge. He printed a copy of the confirmation for his reference. Then he realized that he would have to tell his parents about this venture. Picking up his cell phone, he dialed the number of his parents' home. His mother answered. "Hello, Mom." "What a pleasant surprise, Pat. How are you doing?" "I'm okay. How are you and Dad?" "We're all right. Thanks for asking. So, what can I do for you, Pat?" "I am letting you know that I am planning a trip to Hancock, Massachusetts three weeks from this Friday. I will be staying at the Berkshire Motor Lodge. The telephone number is (413) 555-3476." "Why are you going there?" Pat frowned. He didn't want to admit to his mother what he was doing on the side. "I really don't want to get into a lot of detail about it over the telephone. Suffice it to say it's a chance to improve the quality of my life." Maureen Kavanaugh didn't quite know what to make of this response, but she respected her son's privacy. "I guess you don't want us to know just yet, but you will have to come clean about it sooner or later, Pat." Going to the wall calendar hanging in her kitchen, she flipped to the month of May and wrote in the boxes for Friday the 4th and Saturday the 5th : Pat – The Berkshire Motor Lodge (413) 555-3476. "Okay, Pat. I wrote down that information on our calendar. Thanks for telling me." "Goodbye, Mom." "Goodbye, Pat." They each hung up their phones. During the intervening weeks Pat thought about the opportunity to learn other strategies as a means of recouping his start-up investment in the program. He hoped that at the seminar he would be able to develop additional methods that could be utilized effi ciently. After work on Friday the 4th, the first day of the seminar, Pat walked home to begin his trip to the Berkshire Motor Lodge. He eagerly packed his suitcase: casual pullover shirts and dress slacks, with dark socks and shoes. He knew that he couldn't wear jeans and sneakers, because he wanted to maintain a professional image at the seminar. He also included basic grooming items. Then he locked the door to his apartment and went to his car. Having printed out directions to the hotel, he first drove on CT state route 8 north, a two-laned highway in both directions, which ended in Winsted at a junction with US route 44. He turned west and continued US route 44. In Canaan, he turned right onto US route 7 north and drove into Sheffield,

Massachusetts. While driving through the towns of Sheffield, Great Barrington, and Stockbridge, he took note of the serene countryside. In Stockbridge, he drove past the National Shrine of the Divine Mercy. *I would like to go there someday,* he thought to himself. Pat remembered his mother receiving prayer cards with the image of Saint Faustina Kowalska. *I can pray there after the seminar,* he thought to himself. Pat continued north until he came to an intersection with Massachusetts state route 43, and he followed that. He drove past the Hancock Shaker Village. Then he pulled into the parking lot of the Berkshire Motor Lodge, which was a mile down the road from the Hancock Shaker Village. There were other cars parked in the lot, belonging to the other members from DK & Associates. Pat eagerly parked his car and turned off the ignition. Locking the driver's side door, he then opened the trunk and took out his suitcase. Then he shut the trunk before entering the Berkshire Motor Lodge. Swinging open the door, he entered the lobby and he approached the reception desk. "Good afternoon, sir. May I help you?" the young woman said when she saw him walking towards the check-in desk. "Hello, I'm Pat Kavanaugh. I have a reservation for a room this weekend." He put down his suitcase. "Of course, sir. You're with DK & Associates. I'll have you sign in right now. I will also need your credit card to fi nalize your reservation." Pat took out his wallet and pulled out the credit card he'd used when he was making the reservation. The desk clerk processed the reservation, and gave Pat a form to sign. "You're all set, Mr. Kavanaugh," she said as she handed him his credit card and an envelope with the room key, which resembled a credit card. "As a member of DK and Associates, your complimentary dinner is at 6:00 pm in the Shaker Memorial Hall, Mr. Kavanaugh." "Thank you, miss." Pat went to his hotel room and opened the door by sliding the card into the slot under the doorknob. Turning on the light as he came in, he noticed that the room had a majestic view of the Berkshire Mountains through the window at the far end of the room. The hotel room was furnished with the usual necessities: a bed, two chairs positioned around a small round table, and a chest of drawers under a mirror. The TV set was housed inside a double-door armoire. An abstract painting by a local artist dominated the wall above the bed.

The first thing that Pat did was unpack his suitcase and put his clothes in the bureau. He also put his grooming supplies in the bathroom. It was about four-thirty in the afternoon, yet the sun was still shining brightly above the peaks of the Berkshire Mountains. He lay on the bed and closed his eyes, hoping that the seminar would bring about a way to make this venture more profitable, so that he could leave Delacroix's with his head held high. At 6:00, Pat went to the Shaker Memorial Hall. Walking into the conference room, he saw that there were long tables placed in parallel rows, with folding chairs surrounding them. "Over here, Pat," a voice called out to him. Pat looked all around the room, wondering who was calling to him. He spotted Dan sitting at one of the tables. He had been eating when he noticed Pat entering the dining room. He put down his fork and called out to Pat. "Join me at this table, so you can get better acquainted with the other members of the team, Pat." "Thanks, Dan." Pat pulled out a folding chair and sat across the table from him. On either side of Dan were two young men. They looked to be slightly older than Pat. "I've seen you both at the meetings, but I never had the chance to make your acquaintance. I'm Pat Kavanaugh." "Nice to meet you, Pat. I'm Joe McKenzie," said the young man to Dan's left. Like Dan, his face was spotted with freckles. Curly red hair completed his Irish features. Thin metal rims were perched on his freckled nose. The young man on the other side of Dan had black hair and brown eyes, with an olive complexion. "I'm Tony Mangione." "As you can see, Pat, Tony sticks out like a green thumb. While the three of us are of Irish descent, he's 100% Italian," Dan commented. "Go up to the buffet table and get yourself a plate of food, then join us back here. I'm sure Joe and Tony would like to get you know better, right, guys?" Joe and Tony nodded in agreement while they were eating. Pat went to the buffet display, took a plate, and began loading it with all kinds of food: baked stuffed shrimp, pork chops with applesauce, french fries, and green beans. He also got himself a cup of coffee and returned to the table. He sat down in the same chair and started eating. "Pat, where do you come from?" Joe asked. His voice had a distinct accent, because he was from eastern Massachusetts, near to Boston. "Connecticut. I used to live in Newcastle, but when I attended

Nutmeg State University, I started working in Millbury at a store called Delacroix's Grocery Store. I also live in that town now, on the first floor of a three-story house. I usually walk to work." "Unfortunately, Joe, Pat is subordinated to a very harsh manager, who controls him with an iron fist. He tried to get a full-time position as an accountant, because that was his major at NSU, but because it's a tight labor market, he was unsuccessful. I convinced him that he had to create his own opportunity, and here he is," Dan remarked. During dinner, they discussed various topics, such as sports, business and world news. Tony also spoke about his hometown of Fall River, Massachusetts. "My great-grandparents immigrated from Italy to Fall River, and my family has lived there ever since." "And I come from Newton, Massachusetts, Pat," Joe remarked. "If you both live in eastern Massachusetts, why do you travel to Connecticut to attend these meetings, Joe?" Pat asked. "We take turns driving each other to the meetings, because we feel we have to do whatever it takes to make our businesses successful," Joe replied. "I pick Joe up at his house one week, and he picks me up the next week," Tony commented. "So you see, Pat, they are making a sacrifi ce in order to continue building their businesses. Nobody else can do it for them. It comes from the mind and from the heart." Pat said to Dan, "I see a lot of people are attending this seminar. Are they also part of CompSec Nationwide, Dan?" "Yes, they are. They are from the New England states and New York and New Jersey. Some come from as far west as Ohio." After dinner was over, the kitchen staff removed the plates and glasses from the tables. The entire hall became very quiet as a woman took her place on the stage facing the audience. "Good evening, everybody. Welcome to the Berkshire Motor Lodge. I am Sarah Ann Desrosier. I am going to discuss the techniques that everybody in this room should be employing when building, developing and maintaining their businesses as independent faciliators of CompSec Nationwide. My assistants are passing around notepads and pens. I encourage you to take notes. I would also prefer that you hold your questions until after I am finished with this presentation." Sarah Ann then placed a dry erase board on an easel, and turned it to the audience in front of her. Using a marker, she wrote such expressions as "don't reinvent the wheel." Then came a series of circles with arrows attached to one another. The circles represented people, according to her. The phrase, "duplicating yourself," was sprinkled quite liberally in her discussion. Pat took notes while she spoke, but it became apparent that he couldn't keep up with her rapid-fire discourse. She was so animated and emphatic about the opportunity that her enthuiasm for it was boundless. He resorted to looking over Dan's shoulder to copy his notes. Before he knew it, she was wrapping up her speech. "Now I can answer any questions you may have." Various individuals raised their hands. After she acknowledged everyone, they stood up, one at a time, and asked a question. She responded courtesly and pleasantly. After the discussion was over, Dan said to Pat, Joe and Tony, "What did you think, guys?" Joe replied, "I plan to incorporate her suggestions when I am talking about the opportunity." "I couldn't keep up with her, Dan," Pat announced. "I had to copy your notes while she was speaking." "Well, she was fired up. She wants everybody to succeed in this business, Pat," Tony remarked. "So tomorrow morning, we'll meet here at 7:30 for breakfast and then another series of lectures will take place until noon," Dan said. "I'm going to my room. Guys, have a good night." He stood up and left the hall. "I think I will go to my room right now." Pat said. "I'll see you in the morning." As Pat walked to his room, he wondered what his parents would think about the opportunity he was involved with. He didn't want his father to think it was a get-rich-quick scheme. Upon entering his room, Pat flipped on the light switch. He changed into his pajamas and pulled back the covers of the bed before using the remote control to turn on the TV set. After watching the news, he turned it off and then switched the light off. Covering himself with the blanket and bedspread, he went to sleep.

CHAPTER THIRTEEN

At 6:30 the next morning, Pat woke up and felt relaxed. When he was working for Mr. Harris, he felt as if the world was upon his shoulders. However, on this Saturday morning, instead of feeling anxious, a sense of calm overcame him, replacing the knots in his stomach that constantly came when he was working at Delacroix's. Pat took a shower, letting the water spray across his shoulders, feeling its soothing qualities. After turning off the water, he got out of the bathtub, and stepped in front of the mirror to shave his face. After shaving, he put on another pullover shirt and a freshly pressed pair of slacks. Dark dress socks and shoes completed his business casual appearance. Pat looked at his watch and noticed that he was early for breakfast at 7:30. He decided to watch TV for a little while before going to breakfast. A few minutes before 7:30, Pat made sure he had his room card in his wallet before stepping into the corridor. As he entered the elevator, Joe and Tony greeted him. "Did you sleep well, Pat?" Joe asked. "Yes, I did, Joe. I felt so relaxed when I woke up." The three of them went to the Shaker Memorial Hall for the breakfast buffet. Dan was waiting for them at one of the tables. He was eating scrambled eggs with toast when he saw them. "Good morning, guys. Help yourself and then join me here." Pat, Joe, and Tony took their places in the serving line and loaded their plates with breakfast items: scrambled eggs, pancakes with

Vermont maple syrup, bacon, hash brown potatoes, and freshly brewed coffee. Bringing their plates to the table, they sat next to Dan, who was sipping his coffee. "Ready for another set of lectures, guys?" Dan asked. They silently nodded in agreement before eating. As they ate, Joe and Tony discussed how the opportunity was changing their lives. Pat listened to them, hanging onto every word. While he did not have much to contribute, because he had been involved for only a few months, he nevertheless took an interest in their dialogue. After breakfast was over, the kitchen staff once more cleared the tables. Sarah Ann appeared on the stage. "Good morning, everybody. I am glad to see so many of you refreshed and full of enthusiasm. I am going to have several people come up and discuss how being facilitators of CompSec Nationwide has changed their lives." She stepped aside for the first speaker, a man named Thomas Pelletier, who stood at the podium and gave a speech. He spoke from his heart about the positive impact that being a facilitator of CompSec Nationwide had on his life. He especially expounded on the results, not only for him, but also for his clients. "And the best part," he exclaimed, "was being able to leave my full-time job and work for myself, but not by myself." At this remark, Dan nudged Pat. "That could be you up in the front of the audience." After Thomas Pelletier finished his speech, the audience members applauded. Then another speaker came up. She also went into detail about the effect that CompSec Nationwide had on her as a facilitator. At the conclusion of her speech, she received a standing ovation. During the next three hours, Pat listened to each speaker say the same thing about being a facilitator of CompSec Nationwide. He tried to follow along and take notes, but it occurred to him that they were not revealing any new tactics to build and sustain their businesses. Instead, the focus was on how the business changed their lives. He found himself letting his mind drift off and focus on other things. It was not until after his fellow audience members stood up at the end of each speech that he realized that the speaker had left the podium, and he stood up. After the last speaker left the podium, Sarah Ann said, "It's 12:00 pm. We will break for an hour, and then at 1 pm, we will resume the lecture series. Have a good lunch, everybody." Dan said, "Guys, I know a good restaurant in Hancock where we can eat and talk some more. Come with me." Pat, Joe, and Tony followed him to his car in the hotel's parking lot. As they approached his car, Dan said, "Pat, please sit in the front seat with me, and Joe and Tony can sit in the back seat." After all four of them were in Dan's car, he drove out of the hotel's parking lot and headed for the center of Hancock. On Main Street was a restaurant called The Hancock Diner, which served down-to-earth meals. Dan parked his car in the adjoining lot and they got out of his car. Dan opened the door to the diner, and a middle-aged woman greeted them. "Good afternoon, gentlemen. Please follow me." She led them to a booth by the window and put down paper placemats, napkins, and silverware on the table as they sat down. She also handed them the copies of the menu. "Denise will be your server." Then she walked away. Denise came over to their table. "Ready for your order, gentlemen?" "I'll have the bacon, lettuce, and tomato on whole wheat bread and coffee, please," Dan said. Joe said, "I'd like a tuna fi sh sandwich and a glass of milk, please." "I'd like a meatball grinder and coffee, please." "And I'll have a grilled cheese sandwich and coffee, please," Pat said. "Your sandwiches also come with potato chips on the side," Denise announced before going to the kitchen to place their orders. While they waited for their lunches, they discussed the speeches they had heard this morning. "Didn't you guys find the speakers to be inspirational?" Dan asked. Joe replied, "I'd like to be up there, telling the story of my success in the business." "That's the spirit, Joe!" Dan exclaimed. Pat did not want to admit that he was not paying attention to the speakers, so he did not make a comment. Unfortunately, Dan asked, "So, Pat, what was your impression?" Carefully choosing his words, Pat said, "I found them to be interesting." Tony commented, "Interesting? Why, those speakers were motivating me to be more assertive." Denise came to their lunches and they ate, while conversing about the different points the speakers made. After they finished eating, they paid the bill, left Denise a tip, and went back to Dan's car. He drove to the hotel for the second series of lectures, which began promptly at one. Pat tried to pay more attention to the speakers. However, it became evident that like the first set of speakers, they were more focused on describing the positive influences that being a facilitator of CompSec

Nationwide had on their lives. They didn't impart any new strategies that would help Pat build his business as effectively as they did. Pat found himself once more tuning them out instead, much to his consternation. Then the lectures were over at five, and the dinner buffet was being set up. Pat didn't want to admit it, but he was rather bored from listening to the speakers drone on about their successes. He stood up from the table and went to the serving line to get something to eat. Dan, Joe, and Tony followed suit, and all four of them returned to the table with their plates. As they ate, they discussed the topics addressed by the speakers. Pat listened carefully, hoping he could follow along with the conversation. He said, "I was hoping that I could learn new strategies to build my business. Instead, all they talked about is how it influenced their lives." Dan commented, "These people all come from different walks of life, and yet they are united together by their successes. That's what makes this business special: it's the people, not the products." After dinner was over, Dan said, "We can go to church at 7, and then have breakfast at 8:30. The seminar starts at 10, and ends at noon. Then we can go home. I'll see you guys later." He left the table and went to his room. Pat also decided to leave. "Goodnight, Joe and Tony," he said. At six on Sunday morning, Pat woke up and took a shower. Then he shaved and dressed. At 6:30, he met Dan, Joe, and Tony in the hotel lobby. "We are going to Mass at a local Catholic church," Dan said. "I'm driving." They followed Dan to his car, and he drove to Sacred Heart Church for the seven o'clock Mass. Instead of merely sitting again in the uncomfortable folding chair, as at the lecture series, there was also standing and kneeling, which to Pat was a break. He also followed along in the Missal as the lay reader read aloud the passages from the Old and New Testament, before the priest proclaimed the Gospel according to Saint Matthew. Then the Mass was over, and the four of them returned to the hotel for the breakfast buffet. Sarah Ann came to the podium on the stage and addressed the audience. "Good morning. We will conclude our series of lectures." For the next two hours, Pat tried to stay focused and listen to the speakers make their presentations. Nevertheless, his mind drifted on to other things because all they ever talked about was how being a facilitator of CompSec

Nationwide made a positive impact on their lives. After the last speaker left the stage, Pat clapped, not because he found her to be inspiring, but because he was glad, the seminar was over and he could go home. Going to his room, he packed his suitcase, locked the door, and then checked out at the front desk. Before leaving the hotel, he saw Dan in the lobby. Walking towards him, he said, "Thanks for inviting me to come here. I had a good time and I learned quite a lot. I'm going home now." Dan said, "See you at the top, Pat!" He patted Pat on his back. Pat merely nodded to Dan as he left the hotel and walked to his car, carrying his suitcase. All that sitting in the chair at the seminar had really tired him out. He also felt that he did not learn anything new that would help him be more successful in building his business. He was looking forward to going home. As he was driving on US Route 7 in Stockbridge, he thought he would enjoy an hour visiting the National Shrine of the Divine Mercy, located on Eden Hill. After parking his car, he climbed the steps and quietly entered the Shrine. He found an empty pew. He focused on the statues of the Twelve Apostles that were placed on the wall facing the congregation. In the middle of the statues of the Twelve Apostles was the depiction of the Divine Mercy, as how our Lord appeared to Saint Faustina Kowalksa, with the inscription Jesus, I Trust in You. Pat prayed that his parents would be tolerant of his choice to be involved as a facilitator of CompSec Nationwide. In addition, he hoped that they would understand that due to circumstances beyond his control he was having a hard time making ends meet. It was not a matter of spending money frivolously, but that the income he was receiving as an employee of Delacroix's Grocery Store was not providing enough to cover living expenses due to unanticipated situations. After an hour of quiet reflection and contemplation, Pat returned to his car and continued the drive to his apartment. When he got home, he called his parents and his mother answered. "I'm home, Mom," he said when he heard her voice on the other end of the line. "How was the weekend up in the Berkshires, Pat?" "It was very scenic and breathtaking. I also meditated for an hour at the National Shrine of the Divine Mercy in Stockbridge." "Why did you go there?" "I saw the sign for it on the way to the hotel, and I decided to visit for an hour on the return trip home, Mom." "Your father and I are curious as to why you decided to go up there. When can you come over and talk to us about it, Pat?" "I work tomorrow at Delacroix's in the morning. I could come over at the end of my shift. I could come over for dinner, Mom." "That would be nice. I'll see you then, Pat. Goodbye." "Goodbye, Mom." Pat hung up the telephone. The next day as Pat worked at Delacroix's, he concentrated on the way he would present the opportunity to his parents. He dreaded that his father would ask a question such as, was it one of the get-rich-quick schemes that I warned you about? Remember the old saying, 'A man and his money are soon parted.' I wanted you to have a safe, secure job so you would not have to sing for your supper. After punching out, Pat first walked home and then drove to his parents' house for dinner. His father greeted him at the door with a hearty handshake. "Your mother told me about your trip to the Berkshire Mountains, Pat." "Thanks, Dad," Pat said as he stepped inside the dining room. "Dinner's ready. Honey, please set the table," Pat's mother said to his father. Pat's father put out the dishes, the silverware, and the mugs. His mother served a traditional Irish dinner: corned beef and cabbage, with a circular-shaped loaf of soda bread. Hot steaming tea was the accompanying beverage. After dinner, Pat and his parents went into the living room. His mother said to him, "We're interested to know about your trip to the Berkshires, Pat." Pat took a breath, bracing himself for the worst. He replied, "I attended a seminar at a hotel there. I recently became a facilitator of CompSec Nationwide." His father said, "A facilitator? What does that mean?" "I facilitate the sales of software dedicated to protect the computers of private clients from being compromised via the Internet and I also facilitate the sale of computer maintenance contracts to customers who have out-of-warranty computers." "You facilitate?" "My job is to facilitate by bringing the services to my customers." "Where do you find these customers?" his mother asked. "I provide Dan, who signed me up, a list of my neighbors. Unfortunately, I haven't been successful in expanding my business like the other people on the team." "You mean that you have a complete stranger contact your neighbors?" She shook her head. "Our family does not do such a thing. I am surprised that you would do this, Pat." "Well, I was running out of options. I have not had any luck finding a job that paid more than what I was earning at Delacroix's. I went to a career coach, and he suggested an acquaintance to help me start my own business. The other people who were on his team were all earning a profit. I thought if I could copy their successes, I could quit working…" John Kavanaugh's face turned so red at hearing his son say the words "quit working" that he reached over and grabbed him by his wrist. "No son of mine is ever going to say he wants to quit working!" "Dad, you didn't let me fi nish. I did not say that I wanted to quit working altogether. I just wanted to quit at Delacroix's because I was getting frustrated with the cruel working conditions. Don't get me wrong; I want to work. But there must be something better than at Delacroix's." "How much money have you spent, Pat?" his father asked. "A few hundred dollars, Dad." "Well, we want you to get out! Every time you spend even one dollar on this so-called business enterprise, Dan gets a cut from the merchants who do business with him. I bet that he got a reward from the hotel owner," his father said. "It's a pyramid scheme, and he's making money off you!" "Where did you get an idea like that from, Dad?" "I saw on it on TV." "You can't believe everything you see on TV." "Nevertheless, we are disappointed with you and your poor choice of judgment. If you are involved with this business enterprise, you are not welcome in this house. We would encourage that you cut your losses and leave. You're becoming someone who's not our son." "But I don't understand why you feel this way. I am not earning enough money to pay my bills. I didn't want to admit that, so I thought if I started my own business, I could build it enough to leave Delacroix's and not have to worry about making ends meet." "Exactly what were you spending your money on, Pat?" his father asked. "It's not important for me to go into detail about my expenses, Dad. You believe I only have myself to blame when my expenses are exceeding my income." "I think that you should have been trying to live within your means. Since you are foolishly wasting your money on this get-rich-quick scheme, then there's nothing more to say. If you are involved with those people, we can't have you visit us anymore. But the minute that you are no longer a facilitator, we will welcome you with open arms. I think you should leave, Pat." His father stood up and opened the front door. "Don't call us until you come to your senses about this business." Pat got up without saying a word and left his parents' house. He walked to his car, got in, and drove to his apartment. He could hardly wait until he got home and then he called Sean. Sean answered. Upon recognizing Pat's voice, he said, "Hello, Pat. What's new?" "I just got back from visiting my parents this evening. I told them about being a facilitator of CompSec Nationwide and they are upset with me. In fact, they told me that if I was a facilitator of CompSec Nationwide, I would not be welcome in their house." "I don't know what to tell you, Pat." Sean looked at his watch. "Remember when you told me about your new business? I hoped that you wouldn't have the individual who recruited you call me." "Why was that, Sean?" Pat asked. "Because I didn't think it was a good idea. I had doubts about it. It just seemed a little shady to me. That's why your parents were rather upset with your plans. I must go now, Goodbye." "Goodbye, Sean," Pat said before he hung up the telephone. Pat continued going to the meetings held at Dan's office suite. He listened intently, and was hanging onto every word. He hoped to learn other ways that would help him build his business as successfully as the others in the room. The other individuals in the suite who achieved that elusive success were his role models. After each session, Pat resolved to once more provide Dan with name after name of casual acquaintances who might be receptive to the products offered by CompSec Nationwide.

CHAPTER FOURTEEN

Dan wondered what the problem was with Pat. If the other associates had no problem setting up appointments as facilitators of CompSec Nationwide with their friends and neighbors, then why was the mention of Pat's name not opening doors for him, but instead closing them in his face? After one of the meetings, Dan asked Pat to stay. When just the two of them were in his office, Dan said, "I'm sorry, but I have to sever you from my group. You are more of a liability to me than an asset. Of all those people that I called for you, nobody on your list was willing to let you and me come into their houses. I cannot keep stringing you along. There is something about you, but unfortunately, I do not know what it is, that turns people off. I never had this experience with anybody else, in all the years that I have been operating this business. It's too bad that it has to end this way." "But what about my start-up fee?" "Sorry, but because you failed to complete the training, it's non-refundable. Look at it as a lesson you had to learn. Good luck, Pat." Dan shook Pat's hand and escorted him out of the suite. The next morning Pat went to work, glad that he still had a job at Delacroix's. Waiting for him at the time clock, as usual, was Mr. Harris. The department manager's face had a somber look, as if bracing for the worst. "Pat, don't punch in right now. We need to see Mr. Delacroix immediately in his office." A sense of dread came over Pat as he and

Mr. Harris walked into Mr. Delacroix's office. As they walked into the office, Mr. Harris said, "Pat, take a seat." He directed him to the chair in front of Mr. Delacroix's desk. "Pat, it has come to my attention that you have been involved in some sort of business enterprise. I have warned you explicitly that I do not tolerate my employees having a focus on anything else except working at my store. Therefore, without further discussion, I am terminating your employment immediately. Please give me your nametag, jacket, and headset that I furnished for you, and then please leave my store. Goodbye, Pat." An astonished look over Pat's face came over when he heard those words. "How did you know about that? I tried to keep it a secret. Besides, I was let go from the group, anyway." "Regardless of the fact that you are no longer involved, I feel that I can't allow you to work here. It does not matter how I found out. I have my ways. Just leave and never come back." Pat tried not to lose his composure, so without much emotion he removed his nametag, jacket, and headset and handed them to his former manager. Then he went to his car and drove back home. As Pat left Delacroix's, Mr. Harris suddenly felt a pang of guilt. Now that Pat was fired, there was no one else he could supervise with an iron fist. *We were too tough on him*, Mr. Harris thought to himself. Then he remembered the conversation that he had earlier with Pat, when he'd said, "You owe me a favor when I ask you. It goes both ways. I do something for you, and you have to reciprocate when it is my turn. At some point you will have to do something for me, because I am your boss." It was too late to have Pat return the favor. He was no longer Pat's boss, and he was filled with regret. Pat knew that he could not afford to live in the apartment because he did not have a job anymore. Unsure as to what his next move was, he called his parents and asked if he could come over and visit with them. His mother said it would be a good time for him to see them. As Pat drove up, he wondered how he was going to explain to his parents how he lost his job at Delacroix's. He was unsure as to what their reaction would be. When he pulled into their driveway, the front door opened and his father's frame was visible in the entire entrance. "What happened, Pat?" "I lost my job, Dad!" Pat finally broke down in tears. "Even though I tried to keep it a secret about being involved with CompSec Nationwide, Mr. Delacroix found out and he fired me! It didn't matter to him that Dan severed me from his team." "I suppose you learned your lesson about throwing good money after bad. At least we are glad that you are no longer involved with that business. Something about how they operated made me nervous," his father said. Pat replied, "But I don't have another job." "Well, I'm sure you'll find something better, Pat." "Thanks, Dad, for understanding what I am going through," Pat replied. "I have to tell my landlord what's happening." Pat walked out of his parents' house and drove to see Steve. Pat rang the doorbell of his property owner's house and Steve came to see him. "Pat, what a surprise. Please come in. What can I do for you?" "I must move out of the apartment at the end of the month. I lost my job. I am sorry that I must leave like this, Steve. It's been a cruel set of circumstances." "Well, you are paid up until the end of this month, so you can stay until then. I will refund your deposit. Good luck, Pat." They shook hands and then Pat drove to his apartment. After Pat went home, he called Sean. "Sean, it's Pat. I have some bad news. I lost my $299, my job, and my apartment. What do you suggest that I do?" "Rent a U-Haul truck and take everything you want to keep, and you can move in with me." "It's okay that I live with you, Sean?" "Yes, Pat. I will help you out. Everything happens for a reason, Pat." "I am planning to move out at the end of the month, Sean. Is that okay with you?" "Yes, Pat. Come over at that point. I love you, Pat, as a friend," Sean said. "I love you also, Sean." Pat felt the tears coming out of his eyes as he felt a sense of relief knowing that his former roommate would always be there for him, through good times and bad. During the last week of that month, Pat moved everything he wanted to keep into the U-Haul truck, and then after the apartment was empty of everything, he set about cleaning it up so at the very least, his property owner would not have to do a lot to make it habitable. Pat drove the U-Haul truck to Sean's apartment. When Sean saw Pat approaching his apartment, he opened the door and welcomed Pat by giving him a hug. "It's going to be all right, Pat. Let me drive you to your old apartment so you can get your car. Then I'll meet you back here." "Thanks, Sean, for letting me live with you I have been through. You're a lifesaver," Pat said. After they drove to Pat's old apartment, Pat waved to Sean as he opened the car door and sat behind the wheel. Then he first drove to Steve's house, dropped off the apartment keys, and gave Steve his new address so that he could mail Pat's security deposit refund. "Good luck, Pat," Steve said as they shook hands. After leaving Steve's house, Pat drove to Sean's and they began taking the items out of the U-Haul truck and putting them in their apartment. After that was finished, Pat said, "I'm going to call my parents and tell them what has happened so far." He dialed their number on his cell phone. "Hello, Mom. I am living with Sean at his apartment." "I'm glad that you have a roof over your head and food on the table, son. Your father and I are very proud of you for enduring this trial." "Sean has been there for me through thick and thin. I do not know where I would be without him. I'm just letting you know where I am, Mom." "Everything happens for a reason, Pat. Goodbye." "Goodbye, Mom." Pat hung up the telephone. Turning to Sean, he said, "Thanks for being a friend to me. If it weren't for you, I would have been out on the streets." "The pleasure is all mine, Pat. Now let's you get unpacked," Sean said. As Pat and Sean unpacked his possessions, a whirlwind of memories flooded his mind. He realized he'd come a long way from being a student at NSU. He no longer felt trapped by an insensitive boss whose duty was to remind him of his subordinate status. Nor did it even bother him that Stacey kept pushing him away from her. All that mattered to him was actually seeing the light at the end of the tunnel. While living with Sean, the events that he'd experienced as an employee of Delacroix's and as a facilitator of CompSec Nationwide were finally erased from his mind. Pat enjoyed being Sean's roommate for years to come.

* 9 7 9 8 8 8 7 0 3 0 3 1 9 *